Tales from the Underland

by Dennis Hamley

Illustrated by Miranda Gray

Fife Council Education Department
King's Road Primary School
King's Crescent, Rosyth KY11 2RS

LONGMAN

CONTENTS

Introduction by the Author

Ever since they first walked the earth, human beings have wanted there to be another world, out of sight, as an alternative to theirs. We only have one life each that we can be sure of: how marvellous it would be if there were other worlds where other lives could be led. Our ancestors believed in these other worlds and their storytellers pictured them clearly. Sometimes our ancestors wanted their gods to live in them, sometimes their dead, sometimes both together. Now and again, they thought, intrepid people from this world could visit these other worlds – and even, occasionally, return to tell the tale. Many of the world's great religions include worlds like this, where people can go either joyfully or sorrowfully – for instance, heaven and hell.

Old religions and stories have different versions: Avalon, where King Arthur was taken after he died; Tir N'a Nog, the land of eternal youth, believed in by the pre-Christian Celts. The ancient Greeks and Romans believed in Hades, the Underworld. It was there that, in the first tellings of the story that became Sir Orfeo, Orpheus went, unsuccessfully, to rescue Eurydice. By the time the story reached England, the Underworld had changed to Faeryland or the Underland and Orfeo was triumphant.

Faeryland – everyone knew about the faeries, who were not little magic creatures with gossamer wings. No, they were strange, inhuman, ill-disposed creatures. They were always coming out of the Underland to this world to upset the humans

– and not only did most humans believe in them, but they continually suffered at the faeries' tiny, sharp, little hands. Crops failed, hens wouldn't lay eggs, milk turned sour, lovely babies were stolen and strange, bad-tempered, little creatures – old before their time – took their place.

So where was the Underland? Many were the entrances – under rocks, in caves, inside hills, on islands, at the bottom of the sea, on lonely moors. Sometimes the entrances were clear: sometimes they disappeared, never to be found again. Many of our ancestors buried their dead in burial mounds which stood on the ground like little hills – such barrows or tumuli can still be seen today. Who was to say that, once safely inside their mound, the dead did not live a life of their own and sometimes come out to visit the living? In this way, stories of ghosts or faeries started. Who was to say that inside the mound there was not another little world: the Underland or Faeryland, something like ours but in some disturbing ways very, very different?

So the stories started about the Underland – a place where humans could occasionally go but not be at home: a place just round the corner, out of sight but there all the same: a place of both beauty and terror, of both peace and danger. Here are eight stories of that magical place – two each from England, Ireland, Scotland and Wales. In stories like these lie the seeds of the fantasies we read and watch nowadays: C S Lewis's *Narnia*, Alan Garner's *Elidor*, J R R Tolkien's *Middle Earth*, the other worlds of the fighting fantasies in game books and computer programs. We seem to need the stories just as much as our ancestors did.

SAYING THE NAMES

Several of the characters' names in this book are from other languages – Middle English, Gaelic or Welsh. Here is a rough guide as to how to say some of them.

Orfeo	Or – fay – oh
Heurodis	Hew – ro – diss
Oisin	Oo – sheen
Niamh	Neeve (honestly!)
Pwll	Poo – hill
Rhiannon	Ree – ann – onn
Heyvedd	Heff – eth
Tiernon Trwvliant	Teer – nonn Troove – lee – ant
Gwri	Goo – ree
Pryderi	Proo – therry

Dennis Hamley

Elidor Enters the Underland

What did life offer to Elidor? Not much.

That's what he thought as he watched the wiry sheep on the hillside. Day after day he shuffled out of the little house deep in Wales to look after the few sheep – except when he could go to school, learn the scriptures, learn to count and listen to stories. And what would happen when his mother died? A squabble with his elder brothers over who would have the farm – which he would lose – and then a life of hard work, not enough food and nothing to show for it in the end ... unless he went into the monastery. The life of a brother was hard in different ways, but at least – as far as Elidor could see – it did mean a bit more food.

These were hard prospects for someone who was only eleven. He sighed for better things. He thought of the stories he heard: of great kings and warriors; knights and their ladies; princes touched with magic who went into Faeryland and came out even stronger than before. But such things were not for him. He was no fighter – just a poor boy who lived in a hovel on the hillside.

"You're neither use nor ornament, Elidor," his mother said, when he came home. "You're not worth feeding and I don't know what's to become of you."

"Thin stew and stale bread again; cuffs and shouts from my big brothers; a lumpy bed of straw and shivering with cold all night – this will not do," thought Elidor.

Next morning, when he left the house as usual, he did not go up the hill towards the sheep. No. Something made him turn towards the valley and the woods, the whispering trees and the rushing river.

His mind was whirling with visions of the great heroes of long ago. His brain echoed with the sounds of galloping horses, braying trumpets, clashing swords. He was hardly aware of his surroundings on this dull October day – until he found himself deep in the quiet, dark woods standing in front of a cave which gaped open like a door left ajar.

Elidor peered into the darkness. He listened. What was that noise? Was it the ripple of water over stone of an underground stream or was it light, laughing voices saying: "Come in, Elidor. We've been expecting you"?

Elidor cautiously entered the cave. Soon it was pitch dark round him: the entrance seemed a long way behind. At first he could walk without trouble. Then the way narrowed, the ceiling came down to meet his head and the floor rose like a steep hill. Elidor had to get on hands and knees and crawl.

"This is daft. I should go back," he thought. But the sound ahead was growing louder and saying even more clearly, "Come in, Elidor. We've been expecting you."

Now Elidor was frightened. These were voices: he was being led into a trap. He couldn't turn round and he couldn't turn backwards. He would die here, deep underground, and no one would ever know.

Just as he had given himself up for lost, he saw light ahead of him. Had he crawled all the way to the other side of the wood and was he about to emerge only a mile or so from his home?

The light grew brighter. Suddenly, Elidor burst free of his narrow, rocky prison. He stood up on soft grass and saw a landscape such as he had never seen before.

Green meadows patched with bright flowers ran down to a wide, calm river. Graceful willow trees lined its banks. All was colour and light. Round his face blew a warm, caressing breeze. This was nothing like the bare hillside dotted with sheep he knew so well.

Now he knew whose voices had called him, for in front of him stood a group of people on horseback. They were perfectly formed with long, fine hair: men and women dressed in colourful, flowing clothes. But they were all so small: no larger than six-year-old children. Their white horses were elegant, with long, handsome necks and noble heads – but they were no larger than greyhounds. As he stood blinking before them, they laughed and repeated: "Come in, Elidor. We've been expecting you."

"Where am I?"

They laughed.

"You are in the Underland," said one.

"You are in Faeryland," said another.

"You are where mortals long to be," said a third. "You are where no one ever dies," said a fourth.

"I want to go home," said Elidor.

"No," said a fifth. "You must come with us to see our king. Follow us."

They turned their horses and walked off, down the slope of the meadow to the river. Elidor followed, along the reedy bank of the river where swans floated and boats with silken sails passed by, until he saw before him a vast castle such as he had never even imagined. Its great outer wall shone like glass. The many towers and spires within it glowed with deep reds, greens and blues. Elidor blinked at the sight.

The horses clattered over the drawbridge and through the gatehouse. Elidor followed. The horses stopped and the riders dismounted. Elidor waited – and then followed once again as they continued on foot through wide courtyards until they reached the great hall itself. The double doors opened – and Elidor saw, at the far end, seated under a canopy which shone with intricate illuminations of every colour imaginable, the King and Queen of Faeryland.

They sat together, unmoving. They wore robes of a blinding white, edged with gold. Their crowns were of purest, palest silver. The queen's face was the most beautiful, the king's face the most handsome that Elidor had ever seen. But they were hard, cold, even – it occurred to Elidor with a chill to the heart – inhuman.

"Who is this?" said the king.

"A mortal," said one of Elidor's guides.

"Let him speak for himself," said the king.

"Please, your highness," stuttered Elidor. "My name is Elidor and I look after the sheep on my mother's farm and do what my brothers tell me."

"And why are you here?"

"Please, I found a cave and followed the voices."

"Hmm," said the king. "You are lucky. I and my people often come into your world, on May Eve and Hallowe'en especially. But very few of you manage to come down here and survive the journey. There must be a reason."

Greatly daring, Elidor asked, "Why?"

"Humans may come down here to seek what they have lost. They may come down here because we want them to. They may be performing a task or fulfilling a quest. Usually we allow them to leave again, though they are sadder and wiser by then. Sometimes we capture them and hold them prisoner. Sometimes they stray here, as you have. And then we have great trouble knowing what to do with them."

Now really scared, Elidor repeated, "Why?"

But the king ignored him as he continued. "Humans reach us through all sorts of hidden entrances to our world set in their world. They always come to the same place – yet they always seem to go away with different ideas about what they have seen. Would you say" – and here Elidor realised he was being asked a direct question – "that we are big or little?"

"Little, your highness," said Elidor, wondering why, if the king was so little, he was so scared.

"There you are," said the king. "To you, a boy, we are little. To some mortals who come here, we are exactly like humans so in the world outside none can tell the difference. To others, we are giants."

"And to some," said the queen, "we seem gentle and loving. To others, we are hard and unyielding. To yet others, we are cruel and violent."

"Strange, is it not, how mortals see us?" said the king.

"Because," said the queen, "we are none of these things. We are ourselves and you mortals, whenever you find us, must make of us what you will."

Servants arrived and set dishes of fragrant food and goblets of wine before the royal pair. Elidor watched, famished and envious.

"What would you be eating now at home?" said the queen.

Elidor visualised very clearly the hunk of doughy bread and the watery stew.

"Nothing like that," he said.

"Why not stay here," said the king, "and eat well for ever?"

Elidor stared. What a temptation! But how could he? "What about my mother and brothers?" he stammered.

"They'll manage without you," said the king.

"You can be playmate for our son," said the queen.

Elidor thought: "Yes, it is lovely here while at home all is misery and poverty." Home. He imagined his mother worried sick, wondering where he was.

"At least I must let my mother know where I am," he said.

"Very well," said the king. "Faeryland now will be your home. But I will allow you to go back into the world of mortals to see your mother for short visits as long as you promise always to return. And remember – *never* take anything from here away with you and never bring anything back."

"Thank you," said Elidor. "But why can't I take anything away?"

"If humans enter and leave again, they can only take what is rightly theirs. So either they brought it with them or we stole it, they came in search and we have taken pity on them. Remember that and you will come to no harm."

Then Elidor was led away to a flowery, sunny garden where the son of the king and queen and other faery children played. He was still hungry and nobody had thought to let him eat from the dishes piled up on the high table. So he watched, less than fascinated, the games the children were playing.

They played a game which looked like marbles. But the objects they rolled looked more like apples. They were golden-yellow in colour. One rolled to Elidor and he picked it up. It was an apple. At last – *food*. He put in to his mouth and was just about to take a huge bite.

"I shouldn't if I were you," said one of the children. He wore a silver coronet and Elidor realised this must be the son of the king and queen.

"Why not?" said Elidor.

"Because you are human. Humans who eat these lose the one thing that makes them human."

Elidor dropped the golden globe at once.

"What about you then?" he said.

"We don't need to eat them. Now, stop worrying. Are you playing or not?"

So Elidor played and later he ate. This went on for day after day and the memories of the cold hillside grew dim. He learnt more and more about the Underland. Some of it he liked: some of it frightened him deeply. But one night, as he slept on his soft bed between his silk sheets, he dreamt of his mother sitting in front of the fire crying and when he got up he went straight to the king and asked if he could go home to see her.

"You may," said the king. "But remember – take nothing out and bring nothing back. And you have made a solemn promise to return."

"I know," said Elidor. "I will."

So he was led back through the narrow tunnel, into the cave, into the woods near his home. Then he climbed the hill to his mother's house.

There she was, stirring the pot and not a bit worried about him.

"But I've been away months," Elidor cried.

"Don't be silly, boy. You left the house not three hours ago. Why aren't you out with the sheep?"

"But I've been to the Underland. And soon I'm going back there. I promised the king."

"Out of my way and stop talking nonsense," said his mother. "I've got work to do."

Elidor trailed miserably out of the house. What was the point of having marvellous adventures if no one believed you? He *had* been to the Underland. How could he prove it?

He recalled what the king had said. "Humans may come down to seek what they have lost. They may come down because we ask them to ... usually we allow them to leave, though they may be sadder and wiser by then." And what did the queen say? "We are ourselves ... and you mortals must make of us what you will."

So the tales he had heard were true. He wasn't the only mortal to visit the Underland. Right, so that's what he would do while he was here in the world of mortals. He would find all the stories he could about other visitors to that marvellous place. He would see how these visitors got there, how they saw the dwellers in the Underland and whether what they saw was different from the impressions he had gained. He would see whether the faery folk were loving and kind, or whether they were cruel and unforgiving. He would compare what these other visitors saw with what he saw and so convince his mother that he really had been to Faeryland – and was going back.

Though if time was so different there that she never realised he was gone, he needn't feel homesick or regretful after all. He was going to have two separate lives. Wonderful.

So Elidor searched. He asked the teacher he sometimes had lessons from. He went to the monastery and asked the monks. He peered into their beautiful parchment books with the coloured illuminations. He listened to passing minstrels and storytellers. Here are the stories he had heard by the time he was ready to go back.

Sir Orfeo

Once, so they say, there was a king in England, a high lord, whose name was Orfeo. He was a great man: great in body, great in spirit – generous and courteous to everyone. Some said he was descended from the gods themselves. This could have been true. If you were to meet him you would know at once you were with someone very special – in one way particularly.

Almost more than anything else, Orfeo loved the music of the harp. All the harpists in the land knew that they would gain honour from Orfeo. But they never beat him. Orfeo was not just a listener. He played the harp himself. He applied all his wits to it so that soon he was the best harpist of all. No one, people said, could come near him – and they didn't say this just because he was the high lord. They said it because he really was the finest they had ever heard. Anyone who sat at Orfeo's feet as he played and took in the joy of his melodies and harmonies would feel transported straight to Paradise itself.

Some say that Orfeo's palace was in Winchester. Others doubt it. But all agree about his wife. Dame Heurodis was the most beautiful woman in the land and, like her husband, full of goodness and fairness. Everybody, whether high or low in the lands Orfeo ruled with the help of his faithful steward, thought them the ideal couple.

So the land, it seemed, was fortunate and would remain so until Orfeo and Heurodis were separated by death. But secret, strange and covetous eyes were surveying Orfeo's castle.

One year, as in every year, May came round again. Winter storms were gone: the weather was warm and bright. Fields filled with flowers; blossoms bloomed on boughs. Heurodis looked out of her window one bright morning and saw all this beauty. She turned to the two maidens who were with her.

"It's so lovely outside," she said. "Let's go down to the orchard where we can feel the sun and the breeze and hear the birds sing."

So out they went, through the soft grass and into the orchard. There, all three sat down under a young apple tree. Within a minute, Heurodis was asleep.

"Why should she sleep in the morning?" said one maiden. "We should wake her."

"Let her lie," said the other. "She must be tired."

So they watched and waited and still she slept, through the morning and far into the afternoon. She twisted and jerked and moaned in her sleep and sometimes the maidens looked at each other.

"We *must* wake her," said the first. "She's having a nightmare."

But then Heurodis would be quiet and calm.

"Let her be," said the second.

Then, as the shadows lengthened and the maidens began to worry about going back to the palace, Heurodis suddenly woke. She sat bolt upright and screamed – a cry long, loud and chilling to the heart. The maidens rushed to her, horrified. Heurodis wrung her hands and clasped her feet and howled as if her life were at an end. Then she tore her clothes into shreds and scratched the smooth skin of her face until the blood flowed.

"She's out of her wits," gasped one maiden.

"Stay with her," said the other. "I must run to the palace."

So she did and poured out her news. Within a minute, sixty knights and ladies were in the orchard. They carried Heurodis in their arms and put her to bed. They had to hold her down to keep her there, for still she screamed and struggled and tried to run away.

Orfeo soon heard the news, the worst he had ever heard. With his ten closest knights he came into the room where Heurodis lay. When he saw the sight before him, he stood still, shocked.

Then he said, very quietly: "My dearest love, what has happened? Your voice was the softest in the world: now I am deafened by these terrible shrieks. Your body was once so fair and smooth: now it is torn to shreds by your own nails. Your face had once the complexion of roses: now, between the scratches, it is as pale as death itself. Your fingers were fine and gentle: now the nails are cracked and drip with your own blood. Your beautiful eyes once saw me as a lover: now they glare at me as a soldier glares at his enemy. Oh, my love, I beg you – tell me what has happened and how we can help you."

Orfeo's words calmed her at last. Tears replaced the screams and in between her sobs she spoke to her husband.

"Orfeo, since we first met there has never been an angry word between us. I loved you as I love my own life and you have loved me the same. But it is over. We have to separate, you and I. Do the best you can for yourself. I have to go."

Now Orfeo cried out in his grief. "Why? Why must you go? Where? To whom? If I were to leave this palace, you would come with me – so where you go now, I come with you."

"No," said Heurodis. "I must go. But first I have to tell you how it is."

Calm now, she sat up and everyone round her leaned forward to catch her words.

"As I lay asleep this morning in the orchard it was as if I was alone: no maidens near me, no palace nearby. And as I watched the empty scene, it seemed as though I was silently surrounded by scores of knights on horseback – fair, noble, well-armed. The leader bent down to me as I lay and said I must go with them to their king. But I said, 'No, I dare not and I will not.' So they turned away and galloped off as fast as they could and I was again alone. But not for long. Soon another, larger host silently surrounded me: a hundred knights and a hundred damsels, all dressed in white and all on snow-white horses. I had never seen so fine and handsome a band before. And in the middle was their king, white-robed, with a crown on his head not of gold but of palest silver shining like a precious stone. By him stood a white horse, saddled but riderless. They all stood round me, soundless, and I was frightened. Then the king leant down to me and – in a flash, with a strength I could not resist – seized me and set me on the horse without a rider. Then he made me ride with him, past huge castles, high towers, deep rivers, dark forests I had never seen before, to his magnificent palace. And after he had shown me all these amazing sights he brought me back here to our own orchard and then he said to me in a voice hard and cold, 'Lady, see that tomorrow you are right here under this very tree. Because then you will come with us and live with us for ever more. But if you are not here, wherever you are you will be fetched and torn limb from limb – and still taken away with us.'"

Orfeo listened aghast to these terrible words. Then he groaned, "I would rather lose my life than my queen. What can we do?"

He asked every person in turn. No suggestions came – but all resolved to protect their queen as best they could.

Next day came. Just as the strange king had decreed, Heurodis slept under the apple tree in the orchard. But she was not alone. Orfeo, in full armour, weapons by his side, waited grim-faced, staring out over the bare ground in front of his palace. With him were a thousand knights, surrounding the orchard, facing outwards and keeping watch on every approach to it. "We will die where we stand rather than see Heurodis harmed," they said. No enemy army led by a hostile king could come anywhere near them.

The sun beat down out of the clear sky. All day they waited, staring out into the shimmering distance. Not a movement did they see: not a sound did they hear. Stillness and silence entranced the day.

Evening came. Their work was done. No enemy had dared approach. They turned triumphantly to the tree where Heurodis lay. Nothing. The space beneath the tree was empty. Heurodis had vanished into thin air.

"She is spirited away," said one knight in an awed voice.

"It was the king of Faeryland who came to her," said another.

"She is in the Underland where she will never be reached," said a third.

But Orfeo could say nothing. He marched straight to his room and there he sat alone for hours, dazed, still as a stone. Then, at last, he could make a sound. Howls and moans racked his body, almost enough to end his life there and then.

But in the end all grief gives way to thought and after he could cry no more, Orfeo pondered on what he should do. He took down his harp and played, hour after hour, sad melodies which filled the palace and consoled the people. As his own music took hold of his mind and he saw clearly again, he realised what he must do. As dawn broke, he lay down his harp and slept.

When he rose, full of new resolve, he summoned all the barons, earls, lords and knights to the great hall of his palace and spoke thus to them: "Gentlemen, by now you know what has happened. You also know that I have a steward who for years I have trusted completely and who in turn has never let me down in any way. Well, from now on he is in charge instead of me. He will look after this land as I always have and as I know he can. For now I have lost my queen, the fairest lady that ever walked, I will never look on a woman again – no, not any human being. I shall leave you now. I shall go into the wilderness and live with wild animals in their lairs. And when news comes to you that I am dead, then you must call a parliament together and choose a new ruler. That's all I have to say. My last decree to you is – that you carry out my wishes."

Straightaway there was weeping in the hall; everybody, young and old, begged him to stay.

"That's enough," shouted Orfeo. "I'm going."

He left the palace wearing a pilgrim's mantle, taking nothing but his harp. Barefoot and alone, he walked quietly through the gate and disappeared from human sight.

Soon he left behind the crying and the wailing and the misery of people who saw their crowned ruler of one moment leaving destitute the next. He did not stop until he was in the wild lands where no humans went. He found nothing to give him comfort. He who once wore robes of grey fur and slept under counterpanes of rich red velvet now lay on the heath and wrapped himself in grass and leaves. He who once held sway over castles, towers, rivers, forests, now – when the snow came and the waters froze – had to sleep on moss. He who once had knights and their ladies kneeling before him, now saw no friendly faces but only snakes which struck and animals which roared. He who once ate the best food and drank the finest wines, now dug and scrabbled in the earth to find roots to chew on. In summer he lived on wild fruit and berries of little worth, but come winter he found nothing but grasses, roots and bark. His body wasted away with hardship and privation. Who can imagine the sufferings of this man for ten years and more? His black beard grew unchecked down to the girdle of his mantle: if anyone could have seen him, they would have beheld not a king but a wild thing.

Yet there was still happiness for him. It lay in his harp which he kept carefully, hidden in a hollow tree. Often, when the weather was clear and bright, he would bring the harp out and play it just for himself. Then the sound would echo through the forest and across the heaths and its beauty would draw all the animals and birds towards him. The beasts sat or lay on the ground round about him and the birds perched in the branches above his head and they all listened entranced to this wondrous music. Then, when this charm was in the air, no creature would try to harm him.

Sometimes, on hot mornings when the music had taken them out of themselves, Orfeo could look even beyond his audience of birds and beasts and see, dim and shadowy, the king of

Faeryland himself and his followers, hunting through the forest. Over his own music he could hear, faint but clear, the shouts of huntsmen, the blowing of horns and the cry of the hounds. He never saw an animal caught and he never knew where the faery hunters had come from, nor where they went to. But he remembered the silent dream figures who had stolen away his wife and when his music was done and the faery rout had disappeared, he would lean up against a tree and cry until his eyes were drained of tears.

As the years went by, Orfeo became more and more part of the forest and the world of the animals. The power of his music made him at one with nature and able to see beyond the bounds of mere mortal men. The ghostly visions of the faery hunt became clearer and harder. Sometimes he would see no hunters, but an army of a thousand knights riding strong and fierce through the forest, swords drawn, banners blowing in the wind. But if he followed, they vanished out of his sight. Other times he saw, not warriors, but lords and ladies attired in bright colours, dancing with silent steps while minstrels played tabors and trumpets whose sounds were faraway as if in a corner of his mind.

Day after day, year after year, his music brought these visions clearer and clearer, more and more seeming real. Always he would put down his harp and follow. Always they would turn a corner in front of him and when he caught up they were gone.

One day, he saw a different vision. In the morning sunshine, mounted on snow-white horses which padded silently over the sward, sixty ladies rode past, gentle and lovely as birds on leafy sprays. No men rode with them. Each lady carried a hawk on her wrist.

Orfeo watched in wonder and delight. Then, as always, he followed. The ladies came to a river: there they released the hawks from their wrists. There was game there: mallards, herons, cormorants. The birds of the water flew up, the falcons saw them and each bird dived on its prey. Orfeo watched this and, remembering the sport he once had in his former life, laughed aloud. "Perfect," he cried. "That's fair game. I'll go closer to watch and recall the days when I was well used to this sort of thing."

Stealthily he drew nearer, close to a lady who stood with her back to him. As he approached, she turned and he saw her face. It was his wife, Heurodis.

When he saw who it was – and she in turn recognised him – neither could speak. When Heurodis saw the ravages in the face of the man she knew as king, the tears welled up in her eyes.

The other ladies saw as well. They surrounded Heurodis and forced her away with them. Orfeo again tried to follow, but – as always before – the sight before him dwindled until the ladies who had seemed as real as him were but shadows in the sunlight.

Orfeo threw himself on the ground and sobbed. "Now," he cried, "I have reached the end. I've found my wife but she dare not speak. So let me die."

But something in the strong mind stopped him. He sat up. The faint shapes of the ladies from Faeryland still showed themselves far off. He shook off his despair.

"I can still see them," he said. "Whatever happens, wherever they go, I'll follow, because I don't care whether I live or die."

He hitched his pilgrim's mantle up over his shoulders, slung his harp on his back and ran after them. Many times in his haste he fell over stones, stumbled through water, was buffeted by branches – but he didn't care. Always he kept the shadowy shapes in view. At last, the ladies reached a huge rock set in the ground. They rode round its side and disappeared into a deep cleft. Quick as a flash, before it could close up, Orfeo followed.

Orfeo looked round. Surely now he should be in some echoing, dark cavern? But he was not. He stood by a wide river with steep, wooded slopes stretching to its edge. He looked back to the rock and the cleft. There were none. The ladies were no longer shadowy shapes. Their bright clothes shone in the sunlight and their clear voices sounded bell-like in his ears. So again he followed them.

For three miles they wended along the riverbank, past castles and towers, with high mountains far off. Then they came to a wide, smooth, green plain. Set in the middle was a wonderful palace. The outer wall shone like crystal. There must have been a hundred towers within the walls, all well built and stoutly battlemented. The buttresses which rose out of the moat were arched with gold. The vaulting was decorated with enamelling in all colours. Within the walls were great halls with sides set with precious stones – why, even the meanest pillar was made of pure burnished gold. That place would always be light, for when darkness should fall, the precious stones would reflect as brightly as the midday sun. Orfeo found it impossible even to estimate the riches the place contained. He really thought he must be in a corner of Paradise.

The ladies entered the castle: the gates closed behind them. Orfeo stood nonplussed: he had to enter as well. How? He decided to try the easiest way first. He knocked at the gate. A porter appeared at once.

"What is your business?"

"I," said Orfeo, "am a minstrel. If your lord wishes it, I will entertain him with my songs."

The porter undid the gate and let him in.

Once inside, Orfeo looked about him – and shrank in horror. Had he been let in to be given a warning that would send him shrieking with terror out again? For piled beside the wall of the courtyard were people who had been brought into this place and left for dead. Some bodies were headless; some had no arms; some corpses were hacked and mutilated; some had been strangled as they ate; some were drowned. Some women lay dead in childbirth: others looked as if they were asleep and would soon wake to the morning sunshine except for the pallor of death on their faces. Orfeo saw all this and remembered the words of the king of Faeryland to Heurodis: " ... if you are not here, wherever you are you will be fetched and torn limb from limb – and *still* taken away with us."

Orfeo walked on in fear, away from this dump of the dead. Then he saw, stretched out under an apple tree looking just as she was before she vanished, Heurodis. A chill struck his heart. Was she dead like the others? He bent down to her. No, she slept. So he left without disturbing her and made his way to the king's hall.

At the doorway he stopped. A dazzling sight met his eyes. Under a high, decorated canopy sat the King and Queen of Faeryland. Their crowns shone so bright, their white robes reflected light so intense that Orfeo found it hard even to look at them. He approached nevertheless and knelt before the king.

"My lord," he said. "If it is your will, please listen to my minstrelsy."

The king answered, "Who are you? Why are you here? No one sent for you. In all my reign, I never met anyone so foolhardy as to dare to come into my presence unannounced."

"My lord," said Orfeo. "I am just a poor minstrel. But remember, it is the custom that we seek out the houses of great lords and we must offer our music even if we are not welcome."

With that, and before anyone could stop him, he took his harp, tuned it and played such heavenly music that everyone in the palace stopped what they were doing and came to the hall to listen. Sad melodies with dying falls, wild dances of sheer joy, harmonies such as only angels can make echoed round the hall and through the air outside. The king and queen sat entranced.

For hours Orfeo played. When he finished and the strains of music still sounded through the hall and in the listeners' minds, the king spoke to Orfeo. His voice was changed from harshness to geniality. "Minstrel, never have I heard music that can come near to what you have given us. I liked it so much that I am minded to make a bargain with you. Ask of me whatever you want – within reason of course – and you will see that my generosity matches your wishes. Now, speak, and test my words."

Orfeo spoke firmly and clearly. "Sir, I ask you to let me take away with me that radiant lady who sleeps under the apple tree."

The king stared for a moment, then roared with laughter. "Never!" he cried. "What, you two together? You'd make a sorry couple indeed. Look at you: thin as a rake, hairy as a wild animal, ragged, filthy. She is a beautiful creature, without blemish. To see you two together – no, it would not be fitting. It would be a dreadful thing. I won't allow it."

Orfeo did not flinch. "Sir," he said. "Noble king, it would be a far more dreadful thing to hear a lie from your mouth. You made a bargain with me: what I asked for I should receive and you should keep your word as a matter of honour, even though you are a king and I am the poorest man that walks."

The king looked at Orfeo. Anger suffused his face, then died. Did it cross his mind that there was more to this minstrel that met the eye, that perhaps they were two kings together? For a moment, Orfeo was in danger of joining the pile of broken bodies in the courtyard – but honour prevailed.

"You are right," the king said. "Take her by the hand and go. And may you be as happy with each other as you deserve."

Orfeo knelt and poured out profuse thanks.

"Out of my sight!" the king roared.

Orfeo rushed out of the hall before the king could change his mind. He dashed to the place where Heurodis slept and woke her.

"You," she gasped. "At last."

Orfeo was struck dumb by the sound of the well loved and well remembered voice: by the sight after so long of that beautiful face. He could not move for joy.

"Quick!" Heurodis urged. She dragged him by the hand away, out of the palace of the King of Faeryland for ever. Along the riverbank they ran, past – and Orfeo did not know how it suddenly appeared – the great rock and they were back in the wild lands where Orfeo had lived for so long.

Now the two of them were free. At last, Orfeo could leave his exile. Together they came at last to Winchester. No one recognised them as they entered the familiar city walls.

For the moment, though, they went no further. They took lodging in the tiny cottage of a beggar.

"We are poor wandering minstrels," said Orfeo. "We've been

out of this city for a long time. Tell us what the news is and who reigns here."

Then the beggar told them the story – how the queen had been stolen away by the faeries and king had gone away and never been heard of again, and how the steward had ruled in his stead and how everyone believed that one day the true king and queen would return.

"What shall we do?" Orfeo said to Heurodis.

"I shall stay here," she replied. "You go into the city alone. After all, it is yours and no one else's: you have the right to find out for yourself how things stand."

Next day came. Orfeo, dressed as a beggar but with his harp slung on his back, rose early and went into the city. He looked and listened. He in turn was noticed by earls, knights and common folk. Many were the contemptuous remarks he heard. "What a sight! Have you ever seen such hair? His beard comes down to his knees! His skin's so rough and withered it looks like tree bark."

Orfeo searched through the mocking, unfriendly faces until he saw his steward.

"Sir steward," he called, "a moment. I am a minstrel who is down on his luck. Help me to get back on my feet again."

The steward replied at once. "Come with me. Of course I will help you. All good harpists are welcome here, for the sake of my lord Orfeo."

So, after so long, Orfeo stood in his great hall again. The steward sat at the high table and many lords sat with him. In the hall were trumpeters and taborers, harpists and fiddlers. They played until the hall was full of melody, and Orfeo listened to it. Then all was still again. Orfeo took his harp and played the loveliest music that any person there had ever heard. They listened transfixed until the last note died away.

The steward looked at Orfeo for a long time before he spoke. Then he said: "Minstrel, please tell me. Where did you find this harp? You must tell the truth."

"My lord," said Orfeo. "I passed lately through wild lands – a real wilderness. In a barren valley I found a man's body. He had been torn to pieces by savage animals. Next to him I found this harp. I could do nothing for the man – but no harm had come to the harp so I took it and have been playing it ever since."

Orfeo watched the steward keenly as he said these words. The steward leaned forward, his head in his hands. "That was my lord Orfeo," he groaned. "He is dead. I have lost my king and my greatest friend. What shall I do? He suffered so much and died a terrible death. I wish I were dead myself."

His knights tried to console him – this was the way of the world: death was inevitable both for king and for beggar. But now Orfeo knew he had left his kingdom to a good and true man who had not abused his trust. He stood before the steward and spoke again.

"Sir steward," he said. "Listen to me. If by some amazing chance I were Orfeo, I had lived rough in the wilderness and then rescued my wife from Faeryland, brought her to the edge of the city to a beggar's house and then come to you in poverty to test your goodwill to me and I found that you were true, you would be a fortunate man indeed because I would see that you would be king after me. But if you had been pleased to hear of my death you would have been kicked out at once."

Then everybody knew that it was King Orfeo who spoke to them. The steward and all the others in the hall knelt. "You are our lord and king," they all said. Then Orfeo was taken away, bathed, shaved and dressed as a king again. Heurodis was fetched and the two were brought into the palace with merriment and minstrelsy. Many were the tears of joy shed at the sight of this well-loved couple coming home so unexpectedly yet so fittingly.

Then Orfeo and Heurodis were crowned anew and lived and ruled wisely for many years. When they died, the steward ruled as of right in their place. In memory of Orfeo and his music, minstrels remembered this tale and made a ballad out of it which they called "Sir Orfeo" after the king himself. The ballad is good, the music is sweet – and may we all in the end fare as well as Sir Orfeo and his Lady Heurodis.

Oisin and Niamh of the Golden Hair

Three people walked, one in Ireland, two in the Underland. They had no idea how one day they would meet and see their lives change completely.

In Ireland, Oisin lived, hunted and fought alongside his brothers. He was the son of Finn Mac Cool, leader of the Fianna, the army of the High King of Ireland. Like his father, Oisin was a soldier. But also he was a poet. Strength, bravery and dreaminess together in the same person made him very different from the rest.

In the Underland reigned a king who was also a god. Mannanan Mac Lir ruled his land but also he roamed the sea on his chariot, raising storms, sending calms, sinking the ships of Ireland's enemies and guiding explorers round rocky coasts and across uncharted waters. Being a king and god of the sea at the same time was hard work – and there was another matter which bothered Mannanan. This concerned the third person in the story: his daughter, Niamh of the Golden Hair.

Niamh was beautiful. Her bright hair framed a perfect face and hung down below her waist. Mannanan feared that when she found someone worthy of marrying her, that man would be his rival. He had good reason for his fear.

To keep the throne of the Underland, the king had to run a race every seven years. Anybody who wanted to could join in this race: the competitors stood ready at the foot of a hill near the palace and, at a signal from the king's chief counsellor, druid and priest, they would run all the way up the hill to the summit where there was a throne formed of huge and ancient rocks. The first to scramble up to the throne and sit on it not only won the race, but also earned the right to be King of the Underland for the next seven years until the time for another race.

Mannanan's subjects weren't stupid. The king won every time. Who would be so mad as to try to beat him? So why should Mannanan's reign ever end?

"This will never change, will it?" the king one year asked his counsellor.

Being priest and druid as well, the counsellor could see a lot of what was to happen – though, irritatingly, never quite all. So he shuffled from foot to foot and coughed in embarrassment. He didn't want his head cut off for bringing bad news.

"Answer!" shouted the king.

"The only one who will ever beat you," said the counsellor, "is your son-in-law."

"I haven't got a son-in-law," said the king.

"You had better make sure you never do," said the counsellor.

So Mannanan had cause for fear. Niamh was bound to marry. Unless ...

"Bring Niamh here," he commanded.

Niamh stood before him. As he looked, Mannanan thought, "Yes, she would break the heart of any man who saw her. Shall I lock her away so no one ever will? No, such beauty shouldn't be hidden. But if some young man wanting a wife claps his eyes on her ..."

Magic and shape-shifting were child's play to Mannanan. He leant forward and touched Niamh's face. To some people watching, there was no difference at all. To all unmarried men, however, her lovely face had turned into a pig's head.

"There," said Mannanan with satisfaction. "That should put the men off you."

Niamh ran sobbing back to her room. The counsellor followed her, shocked at what had happened and guilty because it was partly his fault. Once again, he dimly saw the future.

"What shall I do?" wailed Niamh.

"There's only one thing – but it's impossible," said the counsellor.

"I'll do it!"

"You have to marry a mortal. And not just any mortal. He has to be a member of the Fianna. And not just any member of the Fianna. He must be a son of Finn Mac Cool himself."

"Finn Mac Cool? The greatest of mortals?" said Niamh. "Any son of his can pick and choose as he wants. Why should he look at a girl with a pig's head?"

"Why indeed? But if he does, then you'll be as you were – too good, if you ask me, for any mere mortal."

"As no man in his right mind will look at her," thought the counsellor, "I've salved my conscience and the king's throne is still safe."

"To Ireland I shall go," cried Niamh.

She rushed out of the counsellor's sight, sprang on her tall white horse and spurred it on – away from the Underland, up to the surface of the sea and then, skimming across the waves, to the coast of Kerry. There, she dismounted and looked round her. She stood on a deserted shore. As she led her horse inland, she left footprints in the wet sand which disappeared almost at once. She reached a line of rocks with green hills behind them. She waited.

She did not wait long. Soon she saw men riding towards her: three young men, one older. Their horses, clothing and weapons showed they were soldiers of the Fianna. They did not see her as she stood patiently watching them pass. Invisible now, she followed them and listened. Soon she knew who they were. The three young ones were sons of Finn – Caiolte, Conan and Oisin. The older one was Finn himself.

Oisin was the one for her. He sang, he spoke with a torrent of words that fascinated her. He was strong like the others yet, unlike the others, he had a gentleness which touched her. If the others would see her, they would laugh and mock her. If he saw her he would – she knew – look deeper than the surface of things.

At last they approached Finn's castle and Niamh turned away. Next day she waited for them again. She followed them as they hunted, she listened close as they talked, laughed and argued. Every day her love for Oisin grew. Day after day, Niamh was their invisible companion.

At last, she decided it was time to make herself known to them. Riding her magic horse from the Underland, she paced slowly along the seashore as the sun set and as Finn and his sons returned from the hunt. Now they could see her.

"Look over there," said Conan.

They looked and saw the tall, statuesque white horse with, astride it, the beautiful, grave creature dressed in a white robe glimmering crimson and gold with intricate embroidery. Beautiful indeed – but they all, except Finn, saw on its shoulders the head of a pig.

"And what are you?" shouted Caiolte.

"I am from far away," said Niamh. "And I've followed you

through the foam so that I may marry one of you sons of Finn."

"Woman," said Conan in disgust, "what ever crime have the sons of Finn committed to deserve that as a punishment?"

With that, he and Caiolte wheeled away on their horses and galloped up the shore, across the rocks and disappeared into the hills. But Finn and Oisin stayed where they were. Oisin rode quietly up to Niamh.

"Tell me who you are," he said gently.

Finn, a married man, saw the two together. He watched for a moment, then he too turned and rode away from the shore.

"We won't be seeing Oisin again," he said to himself.

Oisin and Niamh rode slowly along the shore together. No, Niamh did not tell him who she was – but Oisin found he was taking acute pleasure in talking to her. Her soft voice and her knowledge of things way beyond what he knew made him realise he was with someone very special. Oh, but that head; that awful pig's head. Oisin shuddered when he saw it. And yet ...

They turned inland. They rode through the night and next day as well, engrossed in each other as their horses led them to the heather hills above the lakes of Killarney. All the while they talked – Oisin of battles, victories, defeats and dead heroes which stirred Niamh's heart: Niamh of beautiful, faraway, magical places which she knew and which gave Oisin wild feelings of longing.

Dawn rose over the lakes. They stopped. Niamh pointed. "Look there," she said.

Something moved in a thorny thicket. There were sounds of breaking twigs and whimpers of pain as an animal struggled. Oisin went near.

"It is a young deer," he said. "Trapped and frightened."

He stroked it and calmed it as he set it free. Niamh watched.

"Why are you so gentle?" she said. "Fighting men like you are seldom gentle."

"Some say that before I was born the Dark Druid had changed my mother into a fawn," said Oisin. "My name means 'little deer'. So I have love for every living thing."

Niamh thought: "What about me?" But she said: "Oisin, you are the hero and poet, the one being who combines strength and gentleness, the only one who can see into the life of things."

Oisin replied: "To me, you are all but perfect. Never have I been so fascinated by another's company. If only ..."

"If only what?"

"That head. That pig's head."

Niamh repeated: "You only can see into the life of things."

Oisin thought: "Closeness to perfection is as much as we can ever expect in this world. Pig's head or not, this woman has stirred me deeply."

He leaned across and kissed her bristly cheek. "I shall never leave you," he said. "We will marry."

Then he stood back thunderstruck. For the pig's head was gone: there stood Niamh of the Golden Hair as dwellers in the Underland had always known her.

"There," she said. "Only marriage with a son of Finn Mac Cool could release me. Now we go to the lands I told you of before."

"Tell me again," said Oisin.

"Tir Tairnigri is the land of promise. Tir N'a Nog is the land of everlasting youth. My father reigns over them."

"You come from the Underland?" said Oisin.

"I do. And now you must join me there."

Oisin thought of Finn, Conan, Caiolte, his comrades of the Fianna. Was he to leave them for ever? Then he looked at Niamh, sitting still on her tall horse. "Yes," he thought. "I am. And glad to."

At once they were galloping, Niamh on her magic horse, Oisin following with a strength he never knew he had. Over Killarney they sped, across Kerry, then skimming the sea beyond the shore until they plunged down into blue depths and finally reached the sunlight and beauty of, first, Tir Tairnigri and then Tir N'a Nog, the land of everlasting youth where lay the palace of Niamh's father, the King of the Underland himself.

Mannanan was horrified when he realised his daughter had fled. Remorse filled him. What had he done?

"I shall never see her again," he moaned. "And she's too far away for me to alter the spell."

So when news came that Niamh was approaching the Underland with a mortal beside her, Mannanan's feelings were mixed. He felt joy that his daughter was returning unharmed: horror that the lifting of the curse must mean the certain end of his reign.

At first there was no talk of that. Mannanan set up a huge marriage feast for the returners. He gazed fondly at his daughter and greeted his new son-in-law only slightly warily. After all, it was years until the next race – and anyway, the counsellor's prophecy hadn't said which race it would be. In this place of immortality, hundreds of years might pass before he was beaten. Oisin might not even want to run. Besides, why should anyone tell him?

So Mannanan said nothing. Neither did his counsellors. The feast passed joyfully. Oisin received riches and gifts he could not have thought possible: a hundred magic horses, a hundred magic swords with warriors to wield them, a suit of chain mail which could never be breached, lands which were for ever fertile, orchards and vineyards where fruit ripened perpetually. Best of all, there was the gift of immortality and therefore a life of endless tranquillity with Niamh.

So when seven years had passed and Oisin one day noticed people gathering at the foot of the high hill outside the palace and saw a track being marked out all the way to the throne made of slabs of stone at the summit, he merely said to Niamh, "What's happening?"

"It's the race which comes round every seven years. Didn't I tell you?"

"I don't remember," said Oisin.

Until that moment, he had lived with Niamh in the complete, careless happiness he had expected. Now, though, he saw a challenge and he couldn't resist it. He ran over to the knot of people ready to race the king and said, "I am joining in."

He lined up with the rest. Mannanan saw him and fear filled his heart. But he was too proud to say a word. The chief counsellor raised a silken flag and brought it down as a signal to start. The king was supposed to take the lead and keep it all the way up the hill with no one trying to overtake him, but Oisin set off at a great pace and was at the summit and sitting on the throne before the rest were halfway up. The crowd looked on aghast.

"Didn't anybody tell him that he's not supposed to win?" someone said.

Oisin looked down the hill. Why had everybody stopped? Didn't they care who came second? Why were they all looking at him? Why had they all started bowing and kneeling? Why did Mannanan look at though he had seen a ghost? Why was the chief counsellor striding up the hill? Why was he taking Oisin's right arm and raising it up as he would the arm of the winner in a fight?

"Behold the new King of the Underland."

Oisin was shocked. "I didn't mean this to happen," he said.

"But happen it has," said Mannanan. "I gladly give way to you. You are worthy to be king. I have had my day and soon I will cease being a god as well. I did a great wrong."

So Oisin's life of ease ended. As King of the Underland, he ruled with wisdom and care for his people. With Niamh as his queen, time stretched out before them in an unbroken line.

Oisin was, however, still a foreigner in the Underland. Yes, he loved his wife and children; yes, he loved his life; yes, he ruled wisely. But often he recalled his previous life with Finn, Caiolte, Conan and the rest. He remembered the hunting and the battles, the comradeship of the Fianna. He pictured the soft green hills, the rocky coasts and mountains and the wide lakes of Ireland. The Underland was beautiful – but was it too beautiful? Was it too easy to live here without danger, without doubt, without question? He was only a human after all and he pined for the old days.

"I would like to go back to see them all, just for one day," he said to Niamh.

"You cannot," she replied.

"Why not? You came to Ireland and returned when you wanted to."

"I am not of mortal stock. Time does not affect me."

"Time?" said Oisin. "What does time have to do with it? I'm

no older than I was when I came here."

"If you were to go back, you might be very unhappy at what you see," said Niamh.

"I'll take the risk," said Oisin.

"Very well," said Niamh unwillingly, "take my horse. Stay one day only. Whatever you do, don't let your feet touch the ground."

So it was agreed. Oisin rode off on Niamh's magic horse: up through the depths, across the blue seas to Kerry, up the shore, inland across the hills to his father's castle.

Yes, here he was. But what did he see? A ruin. Where there were once thick walls, stables and outbuildings, there were now piles of weathering stones. The great tower was broken. Where once there were trim courtyards and smooth lawns there was now rough, tussocky grass. Thin cattle grazed on it.

He looked further afield. Little huts, made of stones taken away from the wreck of the castle, dotted the hillside. In the distance, he saw bowed figures at work: people scratching a living with a few chickens and sheep. In their small fields, crops withered.

Oisin stared. What disaster could have taken place since he had been away? He rode up to the castle. He found his bearings. Yes, the bare, broken ground his horse now paced was once the floor of the great hall. Here was where the high table used to be. Faintly in his mind he heard the songs and shouts of his brothers and friends at their feasting. At the other end was the doorway. The long stone lying in front of him must therefore be the lintel, from which once hung the battle horn. When this horn was blown, all the Fianna would hear and come flocking together to fight whatever battle was necessary. Well, now they were needed more than ever to sort out whatever terrible thing had happened in their absence. So where was the horn?

Oisin looked everywhere. No sign. He thought carefully: then he realised. Of course, the horn was probably lying under the fallen lintel stone. He nearly dismounted to lift it up – but remembered in time.

He rode off towards the huts. A farmer fed chickens: he looked up as Oisin approached.

"Come with me. I need your help," said Oisin.

The man, looking wonderingly at Oisin, left his work. Oisin led him to the fallen lintel stone.

"Lift that stone up for me, please," he said.

"That stone? You're mad. Twenty men together couldn't lift that stone."

"Nonsense. Any one of us could," said Oisin. "Watch me."

With great care he leant down from the horse, picked up one end of the stone with his right hand, while his left kept tight hold of the reins, and turned it over.

"See?" he said. "That was easy."

The man stared at what lay revealed – the great, bejewelled battle horn of the Fianna.

"That's too low for me to reach without getting off my horse," said Oisin. "Lift it up for me, please."

The man bent down and strained hard, but he could not shift it.

"What's wrong with you?" cried Oisin.

He leaned over and reached down, dangerously low. He grabbed the end of the horn with his right hand. It moved.

"Not enough," he grunted.

He leaned over further. He took his left hand away from the

reins and grabbed the horse's mane with a wild snatch. With his right, he loosened the horn still further.

"It's coming," he shouted.

He leaned over still further. But this was a little too far. Oisin overbalanced. He fell from the horse and sprawled on the ground.

The farmer watched, horrified. One moment a young, strong warrior unlike anything he had ever seen before sat confidently before him: in seconds, that strong, young warrior changed into a shrivelled old man, then to a skeleton, then a pile of dust.

With a neigh and a snort, the great white horse he had ridden turned away and was gone, leaving the farmer blinking.

"This place has been a ruin for generations," he said to himself. "Everyone knows that. Why, it's more than three hundred years since the Fianna fought their last battle. Everyone knows that as well. So who was he? Where did he come from? I won't ask where he's gone to."

He picked his way over the broken stones to the barren soil of his tiny farm.

Well, that's what some say happened. Others say that when Oisin overbalanced from his horse and his feet touched the ground, he did not vanish into dust. He changed, yes – but to a weak, infirm old man three hundred years of age. Niamh's horse turned and galloped off back to the Underland to let her know her mortal husband would not be returning to the Land of Everlasting Youth.

Who should then meet and befriend the ancient Oisin but St Patrick himself. Now and again, for particular purposes, St Patrick gave Oisin his youth and strength back – just for a little while. But most of the time he was kept old and harmless, while he recounted old tales of the Fianna and the Underland to anyone who would listen.

Which of the two endings is true? You can believe whichever you prefer ...

TAM LIN

"Och, the wee, sweet, little man."

"And why shouldn't we go across Carterhaugh if we want? The woods are lovely and full of flowers."

"Because of Tam Lin. I keep telling you."

"Who's afraid of a little sprite like him?"

"He's no sprite."

"He's a ghost."

"He's an elfin knight from Faeryland."

"He's a devil out of hell itself."

"Och, you don't want to listen to talk like that."

Janet often listened to the girls who lived in the castle and on her father's lands talk among themselves. And once, her father the earl had brought them all together, herself included, and given them a warning.

"No girl from this household is ever to go into the woods of Carterhaugh alone. I forbid it."

Janet was discontented about this. Carterhaugh was *hers* – or would be when her father died. Why should she be barred from her own land? Besides, life in a castle by a river in the Scottish borders was so *boring*. At least the girls of the household and on the land had a bit of fun. For her, it was all time spent embroidering, playing chess and waiting for some suitor to call who would match her father's expectations.

Anyway, whatever strange rumours there were about Carterhaugh, she didn't believe a word of them. So she thought as she sat in her room and braided her yellow hair one fine afternoon near the beginning of March: "I'll go across Carterhaugh, and I won't ask permission from my father or Tam Lin."

So on went her green kirtle and out of the castle she went. No one saw her. Soon the castle was left far behind as she hastened across springy grass down to the edge of the woods of Carterhaugh.

Under the trees all was quiet and shady. Sunlight poured in shafts through the branches: wild red roses, yellow broom and bluebells were thick everywhere. Janet glided entranced through alternating brightness and shadow surrounded by colour. Then she stopped.

A white horse stood in front of her. Its coat glistened in sunlight filtered through the leaves and its deep brown eyes watched her intently. On a branch next to it perched a goshawk. It shifted uneasily from claw to claw at the sight of Janet and made a strange noise deep in its throat. It seemed to Janet that these creatures were keeping watch over something. She looked further to see what it was.

On a soft bed of leaves lay a young man, dressed in a white tunic. A sword lay beside him. He did not stir, but on his face was a faint smile as though his dream was pleasing him. He was sparely built and looked very strong – but, Janet realised with a shock, he was so small: hardly larger than a six-year-old child.

"Tam Lin," breathed Janet. "The rumours are true."

Now she had seen him, she had to prove something. She had to show everyone back at the castle that she had walked through Carterhaugh, met Tam Lin and returned home. How could she do it? She picked flowers of broom, went up to the horse and twined them into its mane. The horse stamped its foot and snorted and its bridle jangled. The goshawk clapped its wings together, made that same strange noise in its throat and the bell on its neck rang. Tam Lin still did not stir.

"Now he'll have something to think about when he wakes," said Janet to herself. She slipped silently out of the woods of Carterhaugh and ran back home.

She had not been missed at the castle. Her father's brother, the Laird of Abercorn, had arrived. She was just in time to greet him as if she had never been out of the place. Her uncle was very different from her gloomy, strict father: she could always have a joke with him.

"Tam Lin? You want to be careful of him, my lassie," he laughed.

"I'll bet you five gold pieces to one that I can walk all the way to Carterhaugh, meet Tam Lin and come home without a hair on my head harmed," she said.

"You're on!" he replied.

"I'll go tonight. Get ready to pay up."

Tam Lin woke. He rose to his feet, turned to his horse – and saw the flowers twined in his mane.

"A maiden has been here," he said. "And I never knew. Why didn't you wake me?"

The horse nuzzled its face into Tam's ear and Tam heard its words. "I stamped my feet and whinnied and jangled my harness but I knew she would be gone before you woke."

Tam turned to his goshawk. "And what about you? Couldn't you rouse me?"

"I cried out, I flapped my wings and rang my bell but you were dead to the world."

"Then why didn't you both chase her and drive her back to me?"

"She runs faster than a hare, master," said the horse.

"Faster than an eagle flies, " said the goshawk.

"She's different from any who've been here before," said the horse.

"She's worthy of you, master," said the goshawk.

Tam Lin lay down again. The same faint smile that he wore while sleeping creased his face.

"She'll be back," he said.

Night came. The full moon rose over the castle and in Carterhaugh all was light as day with the colours washed out. Janet slipped through a side gate in the outer wall and never stopped running until she was in the place where she had seen Tam Lin before.

No one was there: no Tam Lin, no horse, no goshawk. Leaves rustled in the night breeze; twigs cracked as invisible animals scurried; bluebells, wild red roses and yellow broom showed silver in the moonlight. But there was no one there.

At a loss, Janet stood for a moment. Then she thought, "At least I'll prove I've been here." So she picked three wild roses to put in her hair and at her waist.

With a suddenness that nearly made her heart stop, Tam Lin rose up in front of her.

He roared: "How dare you steal my roses? How dare you hurt my trees? How dare you come here without my leave?"

Janet calmed herself.

"I need no permission from you," she said. "Carterhaugh is mine. I'll come into it when I please and take from it what I please ..."

Later, Janet entered the castle unobserved. She slipped like a ghost past sentries, through doorways and up stairs until she reached her own room. Then she drew the bolt across her door and lay on her bed, looking up at the ceiling.

For hours she lay there. She let no one in. When her mother and father finally persuaded her to open the door, they found a wan, listless girl who, at first, would not speak to them.

For days, Janet kept to her bed. Then she consented to leave it and trailed disconsolately round the castle, talking to no one. She walked as if in a trance; as if her eyes saw sights far different from the passages and halls of her home. Members of the household watched her and whispered in corners. Janet took no notice.

Finally, though, Janet told her parents the story.

"Yes, I defied you. I went to Carterhaugh because it belongs to me, not to the faeries. And, yes, I saw Tam Lin. And I told him Carterhaugh was mine, not his.

"He was tiny, Tam Lin. And he was strong. In front of my eyes he picked up a rock nearly as big as himself. No man in this castle could lift it up to his knee. Then he flung it out of sight. I couldn't believe it. 'Now will you argue?' he said. 'Now I'll show you whose Carterhaugh really is,' he said.

"Before I knew what was happening, he had pulled me up on to his horse and we were galloping away, so fast I could hardly see where we were going. We passed through forests, chasms, echoing caves – and then at last we were in bright light. The horse slowed to a walk and finally stopped.

"We were in a hall of wondrous size. The floor was of pure, shining crystal. The walls gleamed with precious gems of all colours: they winked in the light like millions of rainbow eyes. The roof was of pure, beaten gold. On the floor there danced twenty-four ladies dressed in green – why, the ugliest would have been too beautiful to be the wife of the King of Scotland. As I watched them, they split into two groups and each group moved to opposite sides of the hall. And there in front of me I saw the Faery Queen herself. She stood there, in her white, gold-edged robe and silver crown – beautiful and cruel. She said not a word.

"But Tam Lin spoke. He whispered to me, 'Love me Janet and I'll love no other woman in your world or in the Underland.'

"Before I could answer, everything vanished: the hall, the ladies, the Faery Queen, Tam Lin himself. I was alone in Carterhaugh once more and felt only a desolating sadness as if I had been cut off from some great happiness I would never experience again."

When she had finished, there was silence for a moment. Then her father said, "Janet, I was not angry with you when you wouldn't let us in, but now I am – for telling such a pack of lies."

He stalked out of the room, followed by Janet's worried mother.

Seven months had now passed since Janet was given her tiny glimpse of the Underland. Her misery was such that she could not bear it any longer. She *had* to break out of the castle; she *had* to see Tam Lin and find out the truth about him. Otherwise some faery enchantment would have ruined her life.

The serving maids were easy enough. They left the door unlocked for her one night as the castle lay sleeping. Once again, Janet slipped past the sentries and crept out into the night.

Deep into the wood of Carterhaugh she ran until she found the place where she had met Tam Lin before. His horse was tethered to a tree; his goshawk perched on a branch. There was no sign of Tam Lin.

So, as before, she picked wild roses. Tam Lin appeared at once, shouting, "Don't touch my trees!"

"They are my trees," said Janet calmly.

"If you've come to harm my woods, then you must want to harm me as well," said Tam Lin.

"What are you?" shouted Janet. "An elf? A sprite? No, a devil out of hell. That's what you are, isn't it?"

"No, Janet," said Tam Lin. "I'm not a devil out of hell, though I'm closer to hell than I want to be. And perhaps, with your help, I can be mortal again.

"My parents died when I was very small and I went to live with my grandfather, the Earl of Roxburgh. He brought me up and I loved him like my own father. Twenty years I lived in his castle, until one terrible day when I went hunting. My grandfather loved the hunt: one cold, frosty day we were following the hounds when the sky darkened and a cold north wind blew and chilled everyone to the bone. I shivered with a cold such as I'd never known before. I lost consciousness and fell from my horse. When I opened my eyes again I was in the Underland and the face I saw looking down on me was that same perfect, cold, inhuman face you saw the night I took you there – the face of the Faery Queen herself.

"Yes, I had been taken by the faeries: I have been given their form and am of their stock. I've been set to guard the woods of Carterhaugh to stop humans entering the Underland. Sometimes I'm here, sometimes I'm with the Faery Queen – and it's a life of richness and strangeness and beauty – but oh! how I long to be human again."

"Why should you?" said Janet.

"I told you I was closer to hell than I want to be. Well, perhaps soon I'll be in hell itself – and that's why the faeries took me."

"What do you mean?"

"The road between the Underland and hell is a very short one. The Underland is beautiful: hell is a place of terror. The Underland can only stay beautiful by giving tribute to hell. So at the end of every seventh year, the Underland pays a tribute to hell. The seven years are nearly up. I believe the next sacrifice the Faery Queen will make to hell is me."

"Why should it be?"

"Why else should they capture a mortal?"

Janet was silent. Yes, she knew the grandson of the Earl of Roxburgh had disappeared without trace. And, yes, she believed Tam Lin.

"But why tell me?" she said.

"The Faery Queen has put me here to guard," Tam Lin replied. "And so I do. But also I wait. One day my deliverer will be here. I think it is you. If I were human again I would love you as you deserve to be loved and you would trust me."

Janet made up her mind.

"I'll do it," she said.

"It will be hard," said Tam Lin.

"What must I do?"

"Tonight," said Tam Lin, "the faery fold ride the earth. Soon I must leave you, to ride with them. At midnight you must be where the three roads meet at Miles Cross, waiting for the faery host to ride by."

Janet shivered.

"Let the first company pass. Then the second. Wait for the third. I shall be in it. You'll see me at once – the only one on a white horse. They allowed me that at least, because I was once human and was christened as a knight. I'll wear a glove on my right hand and turn the peak of my cap up. So make no mistake. You must pull me off my horse and hold me fast. I warn you: they'll put any spell they can to make you let me go. They'll turn me into a snake, they'll turn me into a lion, a bear, red-hot iron, a toad, a swan, a dove: whatever I change into, keep tight hold of me. For in the end their power will weaken and I'll be a man again. You'll have beaten them."

Janet shivered with fear at what she had to do. But the prize was great – Tam Lin the elf replaced by Tam Lin the knight and husband.

"I must go," said Tam Lin. "Till midnight and Miles Cross." He disappeared silently into the darkness and Janet was alone.

Midnight saw her at Miles Cross. The sky had cleared, the moon was up and the pure air was frosty. Janet could see far down every road that met at Miles Cross. At last she saw what she awaited: first a dark shadow far away, then clearer – dozens of horsemen. They drew nearer. She heard hoofbeats, the squeak and clink of reins and bridles. She saw the pale glint of silver harness reflecting in the moonlight against the blackness of their tunics and horses.

They drew level. She hid behind a bush and saw their grey, pinched, sharp faces, their hair weirdly hanging in twisted locks, their long, sharp-nailed fingers, their fierce eyes shining silver like their harness. The first company went by. Soon came the second – just the same: awesome and frightening.

Then came the third. But there were two differences. One horse was white – and at the rear of the troops, unmistakable to Janet even though she had only seen her for a moment, was the Faery Queen herself.

Tam Lin drew level with Janet. She threw herself at him: pulled him by the arm off his horse. A shrill, screeching cry went up: "Tam Lin is taken away." And then Janet felt the cold eyes of the Faery Queen on her as the spells started.

For no sooner had Tam Lin fallen to the ground in her strong clasp than Janet felt a violent change. He was a snake: she struggled with the hard, writhing body and jerked her head to avoid the darting, narrow, venomous jaws. Just when she was sure she could hold the snake no longer, she found herself grasping thick fur and dodging the claws and teeth of a lion. A wave of warm animal breath changed and the feel of the fur changed as she wrestled hopelessly against suffocating strength in a hug she could not withstand: she was clutching at a bear. Her bones were about to crack for ever – when she suffered the almost killing shock of finding her arms around a solid block of red-hot iron. Now she felt searing pain and knew her flesh was burning. She was near the end of her endurance. Yet she did not flinch and just as she thought the agony had overwhelmed her, the shock of finding it gone nearly made her drop the little toad who sat in her hand and winked at her with his big eyes.

"I've won," she said aloud and watched the toad turn into a dove which perched on her wrist and cooed. She looked at it lovingly and then she was fighting beating wings, an arching neck and a hard, stabbing beak – because she was trying to cope with an angry swan.

"Hang on!" she shouted, as much to herself as to the spirit of Tam Lin inside the furious swan.

Suddenly it was over and Janet was flinging her cloak over the figure of a tall, young man. In front of her she saw the face of the Faery Queen, creased with anger and spite and she heard a long, unearthly howl of rage.

"The finest knight of all is gone from me and I'm bested by a mortal!"

"Away from here, quick!" said Tam Lin and the two turned and ran.

The wailing pursued them. "I would never have sent you to hell. You were for me. Come back, Tam Lin."

"Don't listen," gasped Tam Lin as they ran.

"I won't," said Janet.

"If I had known how things stood and that a mortal would speak to you on Carterhaugh I would have cut out your two eyes and put in eyes of wood."

"Faster," said Tam Lin.

"I would have torn out your heart and put in one made of stone."

The Faery Queen and her hosts were far behind them now but over the clear night air they could hear her voice still, as it changed from fury to grief. "I would have tithed to hell everything in my realm rather than lose you, Tam Lin."

The first lights of dawn were streaking the sky: the faery hosts would soon have to be back in the Underland. Janet and Tam Lin slowed in their headlong rush. Clear before them now was the castle Janet had escaped from so few hours before.

Now she prepared to enter it with a husband who owed his life to her and a suitor who would match her father's expectations. They reached the castle and Janet went straight up to the gatehouse. She banged on the great door and demanded admission.

Pwyll, Prince of Dyfed

1 Arawn

Long before people counted time, they counted houses and in Wales one thousand homes with their families made one cantrev. In Dyfed there were seven cantrevs. Pwll, a man of fairness and good judgement, ruled over them.

Pwll's palace was in Arberth. He reigned alone, without a wife. Sometimes his people, who knew he dealt with them wisely and well, worried about this.

"Why," they said, "doesn't he marry and produce an heir? We can't risk war to get a new prince when he is dead."

One day late in summer, Pwll said to himself, "I'm tired of the cares of being a good ruler. I need to be outside and hunting. Glynn Cuch is the place to go." There, stags ran through the thick forest and the hunting was good. So that day he set out with his hunting party and his pack of hounds. They stayed the night at Pen Llyn Diarwa and before dawn were on their way to the forest.

There it lay before them, dark and full of mysterious life. Pwll blew a long blast on his hunting horn: at once the hounds sped yelping into the trees and the riders followed.

Pwll loved the hunt. He rode so hard and so fast that soon he was far ahead of the rest. Alone with his hounds, he came to a wide, level clearing in the forest. He stopped and listened. He heard his hounds, who had stopped when he did. He heard the sounds of the forest all round him. Then he heard something else: the baying of the hounds of another hunting pack.

"Who else would dare hunt in my forests?" he said to himself.

There was a crashing in the undergrowth on the other side of the clearing. A huge stag emerged, followed by the strange hounds. At once, Pwll set his own hounds on the stag and tried to drive the other hounds off – but when he saw them, he forgot all about the stag.

These hounds were unlike anything he had ever seen before. They were huge. Their bodies were of a luminous whiteness that shone so as nearly to blind him and their red ears glowed like fire.

Pwll, amazed, blinked; then he looked further and saw the master of this fearsome pack. He sat still on a tall white horse. His eyes blazed and his cruel mouth quivered with anger. A hunting horn shining like silver was slung round his neck but his smock was of a dull, wintry grey-brown.

"Pwll, Prince of Dyfed," the rider said in a deep voice that seemed like the voices of the very trees themselves. "I know who you are. But I would not stoop so low as to greet you."

Pwll was at a loss. These were *his* lands; how dare a stranger speak to him thus? But something about this awesome figure checked his anger. There had to be a reason.

"Perhaps your rank is so much higher than mine that you don't need to," he said.

"My rank," said the stranger, "has nothing to do with it."

"Then why?" said Pwll.

"Because you have been downright rude and offensive," said the stranger.

Now Pwll was angry.

"That cannot be true," he said.

"Nobody with any honour would do what you have just done.

That stag was mine. My hounds chased him; my hounds cornered him. But at the last moment you set yours on him and tried to drive mine off. What sort of behaviour is that?"

Pwll nearly said, "This is my forest, not yours," but he knew the stranger was right so stayed silent.

"I could take revenge on you for that," said the stranger. "But I won't. Instead, I will make sure that you lose your honour in the sight of all your people – a hundred times more than the value of just one stag."

"My lord," said Pwll, "if I have done you wrong I will make up for it. I'd far rather you were my friend than my enemy, so I will earn your friendship."

"How?" said the stranger.

"It depends on who you are," said Pwll.

"In my own land, I wear a crown," said the stranger.

"And what land is that?" asked Pwll.

"The Other Land. The Underland. Faeryland."

Pwll remembered how the white hounds and the white horse had dazzled his eyes, but wondered again about the wintry grey-brown smock.

"My name is Arawn," continued the stranger. "I rule there by right ... but I have a rival. His name is Havgan, the summer-white. He, too, is a king in the Underland and he invades my territory constantly. Sometimes I have the upper hand, sometimes he does. But I would like to be rid of him once and for all. Do this for me and I will be your firm friend for ever."

"If I can, I will," said Pwll. "But tell me how."

"First," said Arawn, "we must make a bargain which is unbreakable. We will take an oath of friendship and then I will work magic. I shall turn you into me and me into you. You will rule in the Underland instead of me but nobody will know: none of my knights, none of my ministers – no, not even my wife, who for a year and a day will be your wife. At the end of that time we will meet here again."

"I agree," said Pwll. "But how will that get rid of your enemy?"

"Because, when we meet, you will have killed him."

"How?"

"Havgan and I are due to fight the night before you and I meet – a year exactly from now. We are to fight at the ford and one of us only will leave. But the person fighting Havgan will not be me. It will be you, though no one will know. You will fight: you will strike him a mighty blow which will almost finish him – but he will not be dead. Whatever you do, though, don't give the final stroke. If you kill him he will rise again and next day be back fighting as if nothing had happened. Every year that happens: I think I've killed him but he comes back for more. Perhaps this time he will not recover."

"Fair enough," said Pwll. "I'll do my best. But what about Dyfed? How will my people manage without their prince?"

"I shall be you. I will reign and nobody will know."

"Then I am ready to go," said Pwll.

"I shall accompany you to the Underland," said Arawn.

Off they rode together, through the familiar forest. Pwll did not know the precise moment they left the mortal world of humans. But suddenly he was aware he was looking at things such as he had never seen before. Set in a wide green plain was a palace with shining walls and broad courtyards, magnificent towers, halls and chambers – buildings richer and more magnificent than he had thought possible.

Arawn stopped.

"That," he said, "is my palace and my court. Now you must ride on alone. Everyone will recognise you and treat you as they would me."

Pwll turned to say goodbye, but Arawn had vanished.

Pwll crossed the moat and entered in at the gatehouse. The rich colours of the walls and vaulting were dazzling. Crowds of servants flocked to him. When he had dismounted, they took him into the hall and helped him off with his boots and riding gear. The wintry smock was taken away and replaced by a shining white robe edged with gold brocade. Pwll was escorted into the great hall which was filled with the waiting crowds of knights and their pages, all wearing the best clothing and most colourful plumes he had ever seen. At the far end, under a high and decorated canopy, sat a woman more beautiful than he had ever imagined possible. She wore the same white, gold-brocaded robe as he did. She was his queen and she waited for *him*!

The richness of this place was awesome. The bejewelled dishes and gold goblets amazed him; the rich food and fine wine deeply satisfied him; the eloquence and grace of the soft-spoken queen charmed him. This was a palace and a company like no other he had known.

But Pwll was troubled. 'This is my palace and my queen,' he thought. 'Everybody here believes that. Only I know that I am an impostor. What shall I do?'

The time came for bed. The queen turned her bright eyes to him and spoke softly – but Pwll turned his back to her and was silent until morning. When day came they spoke tenderly and lovingly but the next night, once again, Pwll turned away and lay silent, his eyes staring unwinking into the darkness.

This went on, day after day, night after night, for a whole

year. The days were full of action – hunting, singing, feasting: Pwll had a marvellous time. The nights were full of silence.

At last the night came for the fight at the ford. Pwll made himself ready. In Arawn's shape he put on Arawn's armour, took Arawn's shield and spear and mounted Arawn's horse. He was accompanied by all the nobles and warriors of the court and as they approached the ford they saw an armed host of equal size coming towards them on the other side.

The opponents stopped each side of the ford and glared at each other. A herald stood up on the bank and spoke to them all.

"Listen, everyone. Today is the battle between the two kings of the Underland, Arawn of the wintry coat and Havgan, the summer-white. Each of these kings claims the kingdom for his own: only one can win. The fight is between them alone – we are here merely to watch."

At once, the two kings spurred their horses on through the shallow waters of the ford and Pwll aimed his first spear-thrust at Havgan's shield. He scored a direct hit: the spear went right through the shield, Havgan's armour and then Havgan himself. Havgan was thrown backwards off his horse and lay helpless in the blood-flecked running water.

He looked up at his conqueror – and knew that it was not Arawn.

"You had no right to do that," he gasped. "There is no quarrel between us and I do not know why you want me dead. But now you have gone so far, finish me off as I lie here."

But Pwll remembered Arawn's words and replied, "One day I may be sorry for this. But I won't kill you. Someone who is not here must do that."

"Then I cannot be king any longer," said Havgan. "The game has not been played properly. If Arawn were here, he would have been bound to make the clean stroke which would let me grow again. That is his nature; he can't help but do it, just as it is my nature to be brought to death and then bloom again later. But he has cheated and put you in his place. I'm finished for ever and my companions have no king any more."

"I only know that Arawn has won," said Pwll. Then he spoke to Havgan's knights. "You all have to decide whether to follow me instead."

"You are now the only king of the Underland," said the knights together. "We have no choice."

So, unwillingly, they swore allegiance to Arawn, for they still did not know that this was Pwll in another's shape. By the next day the whole of the Underland was his.

This was the day Pwll and Arawn were to meet. Pwll, in Arawn's wintry cloak, returned to the clearing in the forest of Glyn Cuch. Arawn was already there.

"Well?" said Arawn.

"You will see what I have done when you return," said Pwll.

"Your reward will fit what you have accomplished," said Arawn and straightaway each was the other again.

When Arawn returned to his own palace after a year away it seemed strange that nobody greeted him with great joy – but then, nobody knew he had been away. But his wife that night saw a difference.

"Why do you turn to me now?" she said.

"What do you mean?" said Arawn.

Before she could answer, Arawn realised what she meant.

'Pwll,' he thought, 'is a man of even greater honour than I had thought.' So he told his wife the truth of the last year.

She listened, angry at her husband's deception but filled with admiration for the way Pwll had behaved towards her.

"There must be very few men like him," she said.

"I said I would reward him as he deserved," replied Arawn.

Meanwhile, Pwll returned to Arberth – which no one knew he had ever left. Casually, he asked his followers, "By the way, how would you rate the way I have governed Dyfed this last year?"

"You were always good to us," was the answer. "But this year has been exceptional. You've seen straight to the heart of any problem, dealt with it fairly and earned anew the love of all your subjects."

Pwll laughed.

"Don't thank me for that," he said and told them all the truth.

"You needn't worry," he said when he had finished. "Nothing will change."

Nothing did change: in fact, things improved still further. The Prince of Dyfed and the King of the Underland had much to thank each other for: they became the firmest of friends. The people of Dyfed saw how close Dyfed and the Underland now seemed: they knew their prince was touched for ever with magic and soon called him not just Prince of Dyfed but King of the Underland as well. But still they waited for an heir and still Pwll waited for the fullness of his reward for all he had done for Arawn, the real and undisputed King of the Underland. Yet sometimes Pwll lay awake at night full of doubts. *Had* he broken some deep and binding rule at the ford in his fight with Havgan? *Would* he be sorry?

2 RHIANNON

Life in Dyfed carried on for some time with nothing to upset its calm. Still, though, the people worried about Pwll's heir and Pwll wondered whether Arawn had yet sent him his proper reward.

One summer evening, there was a great feast at Arberth – so great that even after the first course Pwll felt he needed to take a walk.

"I've eaten and drunk too much already," he said to his followers. "Let's go up Gorsedd Arberth for some fresh air."

They climbed this hill next to the palace talking and laughing in the warm evening air. When they reached the summit, one of the knights said to Pwll, "You know what they say about this place?"

"No. What?" said Pwll.

"It's said that if a man of noble birth sits at the top of Gorsedd Arberth he will either be severely beaten up or see something wonderful."

"I won't be beaten up with all you round me," laughed Pwll. "So let's hope for something wonderful."

"Look over there," said the knight.

Below them, along the highway which skirted the foot of the hill, a woman rode on a tall white horse. She wore a startling white robe edged with gold brocade: her beauty was as startling as her dress. The men watched awestruck as her horse walked solemnly past.

"Who is she?" said Pwll.

Nobody knew.

"Well, somebody find out," said Pwll.

"But we have to go back," said a knight. "We'll miss the main dish of the evening."

"This is more important," said Pwll. "I want to know who she is."

"I'll find out," said a knight who fancied himself as the fastest runner in the realm. He dashed down the hill. Within ten minutes he was back.

"It's no good," he gasped. "Her horse never seems to change pace from its leisurely amble but no matter how fast I run I never seem to get any nearer."

"Get our fastest horse and chase her," said Pwll.

The knight turned and ran back to the court. In a few minutes the watchers on the hill saw him spur the horse on and gallop away. He returned half an hour later.

"My horse galloped, her horse walked. Yet still she drew away from me."

"This is magic," said Pwll, "and it means something. We'll go back to the feast."

They ate and drank well and retired to bed happy, but all night long Pwll could not get rid of the vision of the beautiful woman in faery robes riding the bright white horse.

Next evening, the watchers gathered on the hill again. Again the lady came by, at the same hour and at the same pace. This time the horse was saddled ready for the chase, the knight spurred it on as the woman drew level – but now everyone could see that the harder the knight's horse galloped, the further the lady's horse was in front, even though it never changed its calm, measured walk.

"That woman is here for a reason," said Pwll. "Tomorrow I will follow her myself."

The next evening, all the knights gathered at the top of the hill watching Pwll as he waited on his horse for the lady to come by. When she drew level, Pwll spurred his horse on. Faster and faster Pwll's horse galloped; still the lady, on her steed with the stately gait, remained tantalisingly out of reach.

At last he could bear it no longer.

"Lady," he called out. "You are beautiful and I know there must be some man somewhere who loves you and whom you love in return. For his sake, stop and wait for me."

She turned.

"Of course I will," she said. "Why didn't you ask before? My horse wishes you had."

She drew aside her veil and Pwll saw, close to, a face which made his heart leap.

"Where are you from?" he said in wonder. "Where are you going?"

"I go where I want to," she replied. "So I am very glad to find you."

Pwll could not take his eyes off her.

"Why are you glad to find me?"

"Because that was the whole point of my errand."

Pwll could not believe what he was hearing.

"What is your name?" he asked.

"I am Rhiannon. My father is Heveydd the Old."

Pwll thought: "Heveydd the Old? Who is he? The name is familiar. Where have I heard it?"

"My father," she continued, "wants me to marry a man I do not want. I do not want him because I want you. That is why I am here. I will only marry my father's choice if, with my own ears, I hear you reject me."

"But we have never met," said Pwll, mystified.

"I have seen you," said Rhiannon, "and I knew who you were."

'Of course,' thought Pwll. He knew the name Heveydd the Old from his time in the Underland. He replied at once: "I would choose you for my wife above every other woman in the world."

"Well, if you really mean that, we must arrange a meeting before my father gives me away." She thought a moment, then continued. "I will set up a great feast in my father's court one year from today. You and ninety-nine of your followers are invited. Be there."

"But how shall we find your father's court?"

"I shall make sure of that," said Rhiannon.

Then she was gone. For a year, whenever people asked Pwll about his encounter on the road with the mysterious lady, he changed the subject.

3 GWAWL

A year passed. Pwll and his ninety-nine companions made themselves ready and he led them into regions they had never known before. Eventually they found themselves in the Underland and approaching the court of Heveydd the Old. Crowds lined the way, cheering a welcome and inside Heveydd's hall a sumptuous feast was waiting. Pwll's followers began to know why they had come here.

Heveydd the Old greeted Pwll gravely.

"For my daughter's sake I am pleased to meet you," he said. "For my own, and for the sake of the land I live in and love, I am not so sure."

"What do you mean?" asked Pwll.

"I know who you are. You should not have withheld the blow that would have killed Havgan. You've broken the law of the Underland – that the wintry coat and the summer white should reign alternately. I thought my choice of husband for Rhiannon would help heal the breach. But she has chosen you so you are welcome. I fear, though, for what might come of it all."

"I love Rhiannon and will do my best for her," replied Pwll. "Besides, mortals call *me* King of the Underland so perhaps I can heal the breach myself."

"Perhaps," said Heveydd, but he looked very doubtful.

Pwll sat at the head of the table. Rhiannon sat one side of him, Heveydd the other. The feast started: the first course was served and the wine was poured. Everyone settled down for a really good time.

No sooner had the first mouthfuls been swallowed than there was a disturbance at the far end of the hall. The doors swung open and there stood a stranger – a tall, ginger-haired young man dressed in rich silk robes. Silence fell as he walked up the hall and stood before Rhiannon, Heveydd and Pwll.

"Greetings to you, whoever you are," said Pwll good-naturedly. "Sit down and eat with us."

"I will not," said the young man. His voice was strange, with a sharp accent the company found hard to understand. "I am here with a request. I cannot eat until it is granted."

"Ask away," said Pwll, "What's in my power to give, you shall have."

"*Shut up, you fool!*" Rhiannon hissed in his ear.

The young man turned and shouted to everyone in the hall.

"You all heard what he said?"

"Tell me what you want," said Pwll.

The young man faced him again.

"You have come here to take away the woman I love. I ask you to give her back to me."

Pwll could not speak for horror.

"Now see what you've done," whispered Rhiannon. "You brainless oaf!"

"How was I to know who he is?" Pwll whispered back.

"This is the man I told you about," whispered Rhiannon. "Gwawl, son of Clud, all the way from the banks of the Clyde. These are powerful people. Now everybody's heard you tell him he can have what he wants so you have to give it. I'm to be ruined to save your honour."

Pwll was beside himself with agitation.

"This can't happen!" he hissed. "I won't be beaten by this man."

"There's just one thing we can do," replied Rhiannon. She whispered into Pwll's ear for a long time, while he listened, nodded and sometimes laughed and Gwawl shifted from foot to foot in impatient suspense.

At last, Gwawl burst out, "You've been long enough at your whispering. But you can't cheat me of what's mine so don't try."

"As far as I can manage, you'll have what you want," said Pwll.

"What's that supposed to mean?" said Gwawl.

"It means this," said Rhiannon. "I arranged tonight's feast in honour of the men from Dyfed, not you. So this is not the time for you to have your reward. But don't worry. One year from tonight I will arrange a feast entirely in your honour and then you'll get exactly what's due to you."

"Make sure I do," said Gwawl and set off back through the

night to his father in Scotland.

Heveydd watched him go with regret in his eyes.

"There are those who call Gwawl the Sun-king," said Heveydd. "Now do you see why it might have been better for the Underland if Rhiannon marries him?"

"Never," said Pwll.

"We shall see," said Heveydd.

Next day, Pwll and his men returned to Dyfed and many of his subjects grieved that he still had no wife.

The year passed. Gwawl, once again, came to the court of Heveydd the Old and was greeted with all the joy expected by a future husband. As he passed through the orchard outside the court, Gwawl noticed a band of ragged beggars but thought nothing of them. However, after he and his companions had sat down and the first course was served, Gwawl was surprised to see the beggars walk up the hall and stand in front of him.

"My lord," said the beggars' leader, "give me something to eat."

"I'll give whatever is reasonable," said Gwawl.

The beggar held out a cloth bag.

"Please fill this with food," he said. "We only want to ward off hunger."

"That seems fair enough," said Gwawl.

Gwawl and his servants packed the bag with food – but no matter how much they put in, the bag never seemed to fill.

"My friend," said Gwawl to the beggar. "This is an amazing bag you have here. Will we ever reach the top?"

"This is a magic bag," said the beggar. "There's only one way to make sure it's filled. A nobleman who has lands and possessions and who has come a long way to be here has to step inside the bag, push the food down with his feet and say, 'It's full enough now'."

Gwawl thought this was a good joke.

"That man sounds like me," he laughed.

"So it is," said Rhiannon. "My great champion, in you go."

"Anything to please you," said Gwawl and stepped inside.

At once the leading beggar pulled the sides up, tightened the drawstring and closed the bag with Gwawl inside. Then all the beggars threw off their rags and stood revealed as Pwll and his companions. They danced round the bag, chanting:

"Gwawl, Gwawl,
Thick as a wall:
Gwawl, Gwawl,
Thick as a wall."

Then they each ran up to the bag in turn, kicking it or hitting it with sticks, shouting, "'Badger in the bag': we're playing 'Badger in the bag'."

Gwawl's cries were getting fainter and at last Heveydd the Old stepped forward.

"Enough!" he cried. "We are close to dishonourable murder here. Listen to the man."

They stopped, and faintly from inside the bag they heard: "It's not right for your guest, your equal in rank, who came here in good faith, to die in such a miserable way as this."

"He's right," said Heveydd. "This would bring shame on us all."

"Then, sir, I will follow your advice," said Pwll.

Before Heveydd could say a word, Rhiannon cut in quickly.

"This is what you should do, father," she said. "Just ask Gwawl to give back all the presents he has received and to swear that he will not make claims on us or seek revenge. That's humiliation enough for him."

"To get out of this bag I'll accept it!" shouted Gwawl.

"If you do, then you and your men are free to go without any harm coming to you," said Heveydd. "We will be guided by Rhiannon, as we always are."

"Let me out," said Gwawl. "Then let me bathe and dress my wounds. Then let me go."

"Gladly," said Heveydd.

So Gwawl left with his companions. The feast that was meant for them continued for Pwll and his men.

Next day, Pwll and Rhiannon left for the court at Arberth, to rule Dyfed in love and prosperity – or so they hoped.

But Heveydd still had misgivings as he watched them go.

"This marriage was not arrived at honourably," he said. "Pwll, I know, can be an honourable man, though he didn't show it here. Whatever happens now, only integrity and honour can pull them through."

4 PRYDERI

Pwll and Rhiannon reigned over Dyfed for three years of happiness and prosperity – except for one thing. There was still no sign of an heir. Many in Dyfed were uneasy about it. So the chief men of the realm met secretly in Prescelly and came to a decision. They invited Pwll to meet them and gave him an ultimatum.

"My lord," said their spokesman. "You aren't getting any younger and neither is Rhiannon. We're beginning to think that together you will never have a child. You may be happy with this but we're not. We want you to take another wife."

Pwll could not be angry about what they said: he knew how vital it was to produce an heir. Besides, he was deeply worried. Was this childlessness his punishment for breaking the rules of the Underland? He loved Rhiannon more than most men can love a woman – but was their marriage nothing more than a joke? Rhiannon had to have another chance.

"Give us one more year," he said. "If there's no sign of a child by then, I'll take your advice."

So it was agreed and Pwll went home heavy hearted for by now he was sure the fates were dealing him their final blow for what he had done at the ford in the Underland.

Not for long, though. To great rejoicing, before the year was out, Rhiannon gave birth to a son. The people of Dyfed rejoiced: they had an heir at last. Pwll sighed with relief – the blame was lifted from him. But deep in the Underland, dark and strange forces were stirring.

That night, May Eve, a strange heaviness descended on Rhiannon and on the six women brought in to look after her.

Throughout the long hours of darkness they slept, so deep as to be beyond waking. When the six women arose in the morning to start the day's chores, they found the baby had disappeared.

"What are we going to do?" cried the first woman in panic.

"They'll think we kidnapped him," groaned the second.

"Or killed him," said the third.

"They'll think burning alive is too good for us," said the fourth.

"We're finished," said the fifth.

"No, we're not," said the sixth.

"You have a plan?" cried the other five and leaned forward eagerly to listen.

"One of the dogs has just had puppies," said the sixth woman. "We'll kill the pups, smear Rhiannon with the blood while she's still asleep, scatter the bones round her and say she killed the child in a rage while she walked in her sleep."

"It won't work," said the first woman.

"The word of six proper human beings against one foreign creature from Faeryland?" cried the sixth. "Of course we'll be believed."

So that is what they did. Rhiannon woke, felt her hands sticky and wet, saw blood all over them and over her nightclothes, saw tiny white bones littering the floor and said fearfully, "Where is my baby?"

"Don't ask us," said the first woman.

"We tried to stop you," said the second.

"You were too strong for us," said the third.

"Can't you see the bruises all over our bodies?" said the fourth.

"We were only trying to protect the child," said the fifth.

"But you were in a mad rage and tore it to pieces," said the sixth.

"Don't dare tell such lies!" said Rhiannon. "I know why this has happened and what it means. I know this cannot have been your fault so there's no need for you to be afraid. I shall protect you."

"Why should we be punished for what you did?" said the sixth woman.

Nothing would shake what the women said. Soon Pwll was confronted by the very men who had told him to get a new wife.

"Get rid of her," they shouted. "She's cursed. She's evil."

Pwll knew well they were close to the truth and that the punishment was not over after all, but he would protect Rhiannon through everything.

"I will do no such thing," he said. "You wanted her cast off because she was childless. Now she has had a child, so that's your first reason gone. You want her out because you say she has killed her child. Well, that may be how it looks but I do not believe it. I will *not* divorce her. If you insist, I will consent to a punishment – but only because you are my faithful subjects and I respect your anger and because I know Rhiannon will be proved innocent in the end."

So the wise men of Dyfed proposed a punishment and Rhiannon, rather than argue further with women she knew were liars, accepted it. For seven years she was to wait at the mounting-block at the entrance to the palace. She was to tell her story to anyone who wanted to hear it. Worse she had to offer to carry visitors to Pwll's court on her back. No one ever accepted her offer – but to be obliged to make it was humiliation enough. Rhiannon wearily settled to her servitude.

Some way off from Arberth, in Gwent, lived Teirnon Twrvliant. This man, loyal to Pwll, was a great horseman. His lands, over which he rode and hunted, were isolated. He knew very little about what happened in the world outside. The pride of his life was a superb mare which foaled every May Eve – that night when folk from the Underland were most likely to walk in the world of mortals. Always, the new colt was a beautiful creature; always, though, by morning it had disappeared, never to be seen again.

As the time approached for Rhiannon to give birth, Teirnon – who knew nothing of what was happening in Arberth – said to his wife, "I'm tired of losing a first-rate colt each year. I can't understand it. We keep a watch – but the watchers nod off to sleep for no more than a second and the foal is gone."

"It's the way of the world," said his wife. "You'll never change it."

"That I will," said Teirnon. "This May Eve we'll bring the mare into the house to drop her foal. I'll watch by her myself. I'll be fully armed. Nothing will get in without my knowing or get out again unscathed."

So it was. The mare was brought, with hay and water, into Teirnon's hall. All night he watched beside her, dressed in full armour. At midnight, the mare foaled, with no trouble. A magnificent colt, ears pricked, stood erect before him. Teirnon started forward to lead the foal to the stables – but suddenly he was deafened by a terrifying roar from outside. A huge, scaly arm burst through the window: its sharp, hooked claw seized the colt by the neck. Teirnon hacked desperately at the monstrous arm with his sword. Such was the strength of his blow that he sliced it in two and the heavy limb, spouting blood, lay at his feet. Outside, the roar turned to a howl of pain and rage.

Teirnon rushed out, in time to see a vast, dark, indescribable shape scuttle into the darkness to some lair, leaving a trail of blood which disappeared even as he looked at it.

He returned to the hall. The foal and mare were safe. The blood-gouted arm lay on the floor. He touched it fearfully: it shrivelled before him and turned to dust. He heard a cry behind him. By the door lay a baby, fast asleep, wrapped in swaddling clothes and draped in a white silk robe brocaded with gold.

Wonderingly, Teirnon picked the child up and took it to his wife.

"You have always wanted a child," he said. "Now one has arrived – by what magic I do not know. But from now on he is yours."

His wife took the baby and looked at it.

"Newborn," she said. "But very big and strong for such age as he has. And his robe – he is the child of nobles or faeries. Until we know the truth about him, I'll raise him as my own."

They called the baby Gwri of the Golden Hair and watched his progress with amazement. When he was one he could walk and talk and fight three-year-olds. When he was two, he was bigger than other boys of six. When he was four, he was working harder than the stable-lads and riding horses like a full-grown man.

"We must give him for his own the colt that arrived the same night as he did," said Teirnon's wife. "In days to come, stories will be told about the two of them, for they must have faery blood in their veins."

However Teirnon was hearing other stories from passing travellers who had been to Pwll's court. He had known Pwll well once because as a young man he had lived at Arberth. It took him a long time to piece together the full story of Rhiannon's loss and punishment, but when he had he looked carefully at Gwri. He could not deny there was an unmistakable look of Pwll about him.

"He has to go back," said Teirnon. "If we keep him, we risk being found out and punished. It we return him, we may be rewarded. But whether we are or not doesn't matter to me because we will have done the right thing."

His wife sorrowfully agreed – "For all that I love Gwri, even if he is from the Underland."

So next day Teirnon set off with Gwri and they rode through valleys and forests to Arberth and when they reached Pwll's palace they saw a sorrowful figure sitting hunched by the mounting-block. As they drew near, the figure rose to its feet. Teirnon could see the lovely face that must have been there before gauntness and pallor overtook it.

"Stop there," said Rhiannon. "I must carry each of you in turn into the palace as a punishment. But first I must tell you the story of how I earned my punishment, for it is said I killed my own son with my bare hands."

"I will not let you carry me," said Teirnon.

"Nor will I," said Gwri.

"We have come to tell you the end of your story," said Teirnon.

Rhiannon looked at the fully-grown boy standing in front of her. She saw Pwll in his face and she saw herself as well.

"It is you," she said and fainted clean away.

The news spread quickly. Pwll and Teirnon, old comrades were overjoyed to meet each other again.

When Rhiannon had recovered and came to join them, Pwll said, "My love, at last you may look at your own son. I and everyone else must be ashamed that we listened to liars."

"Now all my cares are gone," said Rhiannon.

"What is the boy's name?" asked Pwll.

"Gwri of the Golden Hair."

"Now he's Prince-elect he must have a new name," said Pwll.

"How about 'Pryderi'? Rhiannon said all her cares were gone. Well, 'Pryderi' means 'care' – so he will carry his value in his name because no one will ever forget what we went through to arrive at this happy time."

So a great feast was called. Joy without question ruled. Dyfed had its heir and Pwll and Rhiannon could live in the peaceful love they had always craved. For at last, with the union – touched with magic – of Pwll and Rhiannon, the story which started the day Pwll met Arawn in the forest was over: the breach in the Underland was healed and the world of mortals could live in harmony with it. The healers were a man and woman of integrity and honour – Teirnon and his wife – just as Heveydd had said.

When Pwll and Rhiannon were dead, Pryderi the magic prince brought honour to himself, his land and his people. Many wonderful stories were told about him and his horse – just as Teirnon's wife had foretold when he was still Gwri of the Golden Hair.

THE FARMHOUSE ON SELENA MOOR

Deep in the West, where the land narrows down to a rocky point and Faeryland is never far away, was a stretch of wild country called Selena Moor. No other part of strange, haunted Cornwall was as close to the Underland as this.

In a fertile valley next to Selena Moor lived Master William Noy, who tilled his land, reared his stock and brooded on his past. His neighbours knew him for a good but gloomy man and they knew why. Master Noy had suffered a loss from which he could never recover.

Grace Hutchens was dead. There could be no other girl for Master Noy. After harvest they were to be wed: everybody knew and all was arranged. The day before the wedding Grace's body was found lying on the moor ... not a mark on her; a smile of joy still on her face; the plum she was eating still in her hand. How could this laughing girl of eighteen be struck down as she ran and be dead but still smiling?

Master Noy stood stock-still at the graveside as she was buried and did not shed a tear. Neighbours watched him and worried.

"The dear man's dead with her," they said to each other.

But no, Master Noy was not dead. He still tilled his land and reared his stock. He still passed the time of day and enjoyed a good drink. But he was distant and seemed to care more about his animals and the wild birds around him than the neighbours who watched him so attentively.

"The dear man's in a world of his own," the neighbours said.

"Yes, I am," said Master Noy to himself.

A cloud of birds seemed to follow him round his land and even into his house. Did they somehow know his plight? Most of all, a little hen robin flew round him – so close that she would perch on his shoulder or hop across the table as he ate. Then Master Noy would be soothed and at peace, for he felt the true companionship of living things. The vision of Grace became very clear in his mind and he was consoled.

Years passed. Harvest was here again and safely gathered in. Next night would see the great harvest supper: feasting, drinking and dancing all night through and no one asleep until daylight.

"I'll order the drink," said Master Noy. People were glad to see him taking interest again. "It's the least I can do. I'll ride across to the inn on the moor today. Mind you come after me and collect it, though."

So it was arranged and everyone saw Master Noy set out on his horse. Then they hurried back to their own affairs.

Master Noy reached the inn and placed his order. Next day, the neighbours brought the drink back. But Master Noy was not to be found: not at the inn, not in his house, not on the moor.

Some were worried. Others said, "He's shut himself away somewhere to brood. He won't come to any harvest supper, the gloomy old misery. Let him fester on his own – he'll not stop us enjoying ourselves."

So the supper went on without Master Noy and for a while everyone forgot him.

Next morning, nobody was in a fit state to remember him. The day after, woken by howling dogs and the lowing of unmilked cows, someone shook the cobwebs out of his brain and said, "Where's Master Noy?"

Feeling guilty, the neighbours went to his house and knocked on the door. No answer. They lifted the latch and went in. The house was deserted.

"He's gone," said one.

"He'll be dead, like Grace before him," muttered another.

"We must search the moor," cried a third and everyone agreed.

For three days they combed Selena Moor and the lands round it. Not a sign did they find of Master William Noy.

Yes, Master Noy had left the inn as he should have done. The innkeeper knew it.

"I told him to be careful," he said. "There's treacherous boglands on the moor: people have disappeared in them before now. 'I know the moor like I know my kitchen table,' he said. 'Don't you fret about me.' And off he went. I saw him and his horse trot off into the moor and it looks like that's the last anyone's going to see of him."

Master Noy's horse had picked its way surefootedly as the sun went down over Selena Moor. Master Noy was lost in his own thoughts and never noticed that his horse had been walking for hours longer than it should have done. Suddenly, he returned to consciousness. Dusk made everything dim and unreal: he looked around in the half-light to see where he was.

He recognised nothing. He was in a place completely strange to him. A low hill to his right, a stream to his left – he had never seen either of them before.

He turned his horse to retrace his steps. The horse walked

steadily back the way they had come. After an hour, Master Noy looked round again. A low hill to his right, a stream to his left – they had completed a circle and he was back where he started.

Three times this happened, until the darkness was so profound as to feel like a velvet cover on his face. Then Master Noy stopped his horse, thought of lost tracks and dangerous bogs which could cruelly trap horses and riders. He said aloud, "What shall I do? I can't go a single step further."

For some time, horse and rider stood stock-still in the silence. Then Master Noy became aware of a glow in the sky ahead of him. He strained his eyes to see: then he was aware of sound. Faint but clear through the night air came singing, laughing, the rhythm of dancing feet – faraway sound carried surely to his ears.

"I'm close after all. The harvest supper is on and I'll not be late," cried Master Noy and urged his horse towards the light and laughter.

But his horse seemed unwilling to go. It managed a few paces, then stubbornly resisted Master Noy's attempts to make it step further.

"Come on," urged Master Noy. In reply, his horse whinnied with fright.

"Daft creature!" said Master Noy. "I'll go on my own."

He dismounted and tied the horse to a scrubby thornbush. Then he stumbled on alone towards the celebrations.

The light grew brighter, the sounds louder. Soon the light was as clear as day itself. Master Noy found himself crossing a lush meadow richer than anything he knew round Selena Moor. Then he reached the bank of a wide river which was unknown to him and found himself inside an orchard. Trees groaned with the weight of apples, pears and plums. Master Noy looked round in surprise.

"I didn't know any of my neighbours had an orchard like this," he said to himself.

He passed through the orchard to where the noise was at its loudest and the light was brightest. In front of him was a large farmhouse surrounded by trees and bowers bright with flowers. This house was bigger, better built, better roofed than any he knew throughout Cornwall. In the courtyard outside it were long trestle tables: at these tables sat hundreds of people he had never seen before, drinking, eating and laughing. In a cleared space between the tables, couples danced to the music of fiddles, pipes and tabors – wild and rhythmic. Master Noy stopped and watched, entranced.

Yes, there had been a good harvest here all right. The tables were lined with bowls of fruit, loaves and cakes. Joints of beef, mutton and gammon were there to be carved at will; geese, ducks and chickens as well. Jugs of beer and cider were everywhere. Master Noy had stumbled on a place where hunger and thirst were unheard of and he had no idea where it was.

The clothes of these people – rainbow colours, rich cloth: far away from the serviceable rags he knew. What a land he had found!

Yet there was something wrong. What was it? Master Noy stared. Of course. Everything he could see was so small: the tables and benches, the jugs and bowls, the people themselves – all hardly half the size of himself and the world he knew. And there was more. He heard laughter, yes – but it was not joyful, generous mirth like that of his neighbours. There was a meanness in it: cackling and derisive. He looked at the faces.

They were pinched, spiteful: thin lips, pebbly eyes, baleful looks despite the grins.

Master Noy shivered and thought: "Where have I come to?"

Then he realised how hungry he was and how much he would like a slice of that beef and a mug of that rich brown ale being consumed so freely before him. Who could he ask to join in this feast? He looked round to see if he could find a servant.

A girl, taller than the rest, was bringing a new barrel of beer from the house. He watched her as she set it up and tapped it; she turned and saw him.

He walked toward her. He was just about to say, "Can I have something to eat and drink, please?" when she spoke first.

"Follow me into the orchard."

Wonderingly, he did so. He followed this slim, silent figure in white away from the feast until they were under the laden trees he had just left. Then the girl turned to him. He looked her full in the face as scales seemed to fall from his eyes. He was looking at Grace Hutchens.

Thunderstruck, he stared. Then – "Grace," he murmured and reached towards her. She flinched.

"No," she said. "You mustn't touch me."

"Why not?" he cried in anguish.

"Oh, William," she said. "I've watched and waited for you for so long. I knew you would come here in the end. I had to make sure I saw you at once, to warn you. Touch nothing and eat nothing here – or you'll be as I am."

"But I want to be as you are," shouted Master Noy.

"No, you don't. Be quite certain of that."

Master Noy, stepped back, defeated.

"Tell me, then," he said.

"I'm here because of my love for you, William," Grace replied. "You thought I was dead: you found a body. No, it was not my body you found. It was a changeling form left by the faeries when they knew I was theirs."

"Ah," said Master Noy. "The fairies. Of course. But how could you have joined them through love of me?" Distress was overpowering him.

"Grace, where are you?" Shouts came from the house. "This barrel's empty. Set up more. Quick!"

"I must go," whispered Grace. "I'll be back. Then I'll tell you everything. Stay hidden – and don't eat any fruit from these trees."

"Bring me a glass of cider," pleaded Master Noy. "That won't do any harm, surely?"

"*It will!*" hissed Grace and was gone.

Master Noy waited impatiently. Several times he could hardly resist reaching out for a rosy apple or a dark and velvet plum, but the memory of Grace's insistent voice checked him.

At last she returned.

"How could it be through love of me that you are here?" Master Noy demanded.

"I remember so well," Grace replied. "Everything for the wedding was arranged. But work went on and we had lost a sheep on Selena Moor so I was sent to look for it. Dusk was falling, I couldn't find the sheep and I wasn't sure where I was. Then I heard your voice: you were calling to your dogs."

"I remember that as well," groaned Master Noy. "If only I had known you were so close."

" 'At last I know where I am,' I thought. So I ran towards your voice. But it never seemed to come any nearer. I ran and ran and got no closer to you. I looked round: I didn't recognise anything. I ran through wild, rocky places, through boggy, marshy swamps, through tracts of land where huge ferns met over my head. Then at last I didn't hear your voice any more. Instead, there was music and I found myself in a marvellous orchard – this one. I was so hungry. I saw a huge plum hanging from a branch level with my face. I picked it and bit into it. But it wasn't sweet and juicy: it was foul and bitter and turned to slime in my mouth. Then I must have dropped in a faint. When I came to, I was surrounded by the little people you saw at the feast. Their shrill laughter filled my ears. The music had stopped. I sat up – and found out what my fate was."

"Your fate?" said Master Noy.

"To be their servant for ever. I ate their fruit. I can never leave now – not in human form, anyway. No. I have to fetch and carry for them and be like a slave with no escape."

"No escape at all?" said Master Noy.

"No, only that now I am of faery stock, I can do faery magic," said Grace. "I can turn myself into a bird – a little hen robin – and come to see you sometimes."

"A hen robin ..." said Master Noy.

"Grace, Grace, more barrels!" The shrieks were insistent.

"I must go again," she said.

Alone once more, Mr Noy paced the orchard agitatedly. Surely he could do something. He racked his brains for things he knew about the faeries. Only one could he remember, told him by his grandmother years before. To avert faery magic, take off your coat, turn it inside out and hold it before you and in front of them.

"I'll try it," he said aloud.

He struggled out of his jerkin and turned it inside out. When Grace came back he called to her, "Stand by me, Grace. We'll leave together."

He pulled her towards him even as she screamed again, "You mustn't touch me!" He held the inside-out jerkin in front of him and turned to where the lights, music and feasting went on unceasing.

"I've turned my coat against you," he shouted. "Grace is mine, not yours. Let's see what you can do about it."

The laughter from the feast rose suddenly like devils' glee, then cut itself off short. The orchard, the lights, Grace herself – vanished. For a moment, Master Noy stood alone in pitch darkness. Then he fell to the ground in a dead faint.

The neighbours had searched for three days without success.

"He's disappeared in the mire, him and his horse as well," said one. "We may as well give up."

They were at the very edge of Selena Moor, miles from their homes. They turned sadly back and had trudged for half a mile when someone said, "Look over there."

A horse was tethered to a thornbush. It grazed the short, thin grass and looked up as the neighbours approached.

"It's his," said one. "It's Master Noy's."

They untethered it.

"See where it leads us," said another.

The horse trotted confidently along a rough track until it reached an old, ruined barn.

"What's here, then?" said a third.

The neighbours entered. Master Noy's body was stretched

face down on the ground.

"He's dead," said one and turned him over.

"He's not. He's breathing," said another.

"Wake up, Master Noy," said a third.

Master Noy's eyes opened.

"Grace?" he said.

"Poor man, she's dead and gone these many years."

"I've seen her," he said and told them his story.

"His wits are turned at last," the neighbours said among themselves. But to Master Noy they said, "Come on with us. It's time to go home."

So Master Noy came back to his house and told his story again and again to anyone who would listen. Many did, but few believed and Master Noy grew gloomier and gloomier as the days went by. Sometimes he looked at his neighbours and his eyes seemed to say, "I am not of you any more. We have nothing left to say to each other."

So he shut himself away for longer and longer periods. Always he saw to his land and his stock, but he asked help of no one and gave none in return. Soon the neighbours said, "Well, if that's how he wants it, let him get on with it." So Master Noy almost disappeared from view as he lived like a hermit.

Six months passed. Then, one morning, the neighbours were once again woken up by the howling of dogs and the lowing of unmilked cows and when they entered his house and called for Master Noy they received no answer.

So they searched – and there in the kitchen they found Master Noy sitting at his table, stone dead.

There was a smile on his face, though, and in front of him on the table was the body – completely unmarked and perfect in death as it was in life – of a little hen robin.

King O'Hara's Youngest Daughter

Years ago, a king lived in Desmond in Ireland and his name was King Coluath O'Hara. This king had, besides his queen and his kingdom, four great responsibilities. One of them, he was sure, would some day lead him into deep trouble. The first responsibility was a magic cloak which came from who knows where and had been handed down the generations. It gave great power to anyone who put it on so it had to be used very carefully. The other three responsibilities were his daughters.

One day, King Coluath O'Hara and his queen had to go away to sort out some royal business. The king's last words to his daughters were: "*Don't* interfere with my magic cloak."

"So, as soon as they were out of sight, the eldest daughter said, "Where is it?"

She was tired of living in her parents' castle and wanted freedom. The only way she could think of to get it was to find a husband and live in his castle.

She found the magic cloak in the king's wardrobe, put it on and said: "I wish for the most handsome man in Ireland to be my husband."

The result was amazing. No sooner had she put the cloak back than a golden coach with two black horses and two white horses pulled up outside the castle. A man got out – undoubtedly the most handsome in all Ireland – and called, "Where is the king's eldest daughter?"

She rushed downstairs, jumped in the coach and was married by evening.

The second daughter saw what happened.

"I want some of this," she said and went upstairs to find the cloak. She put it on, said, "Bring me the second most handsome man in Ireland," took it off and waited.

Not for long. A slightly smaller golden coach with four brown horses pulled up outside and a man nearly as handsome as the first called out, "Where is the king's second daughter?"

"Where do you think?" she answered, was in the coach in a flash and was also married by evening.

The third daughter's name was Kathleen and she was not as discontented or impatient as her sisters. However, she didn't see why the cloak shouldn't give her something as well. Now she was alone in the castle, she went upstairs, put the cloak on and said, "I want the finest and most faithful dog in all the world."

And there he was, sitting outside the door. He was a noble creature, part greyhound, part wolfhound, with soft brown, intelligent eyes – and pure white. When he saw Kathleen he barked with delight and bounded away and she joyfully followed him.

The eldest daughter was now married and at home in her new castle. Daylight was fading fast: night had not yet come. Her new husband asked her a question.

"My love," he said, "during the daytime, do you want me to be as I am now or as I am at night?"

"What a daft question," thought the eldest daughter, and answered,

"As you are now, of course."

"Night is here now," said the husband and before her eyes changed into a stag.

Meanwhile the second daughter in her new castle was being asked the same question. She too thought it was foolish and gave the same answer. Before her eyes, her husband turned into a seal.

Both daughters had the same thought at the same moment – I didn't bargain for this.

When King O'Hara came home the servants told him what had happened. He was furious, until Queen O'Hara calmed him down.

"At least the two eldest ones have got themselves rich husbands," she said. "But that Kathleen, only wanting a dog. I always knew she was soft in the head."

But Kathleen had followed her dog to another castle and when they reached it the dog turned to her and asked the very same question. Kathleen saw nothing foolish in it as she gave the same answer as her sisters.

"Night is here," said the white dog and before her eyes turned into the most handsome man not only in all Ireland but in the whole world.

A year passed. Kathleen loved her strange husband, both as dog and as man. She never questioned him, for she knew there was a secret beyond her understanding which she would find out about all in good time. And she was so happy when, after a year, she gave birth to a son.

However, her husband did not seem so happy. One week after the birth, just before morning came and he turned into a dog for the day, he spoke: "If anything should happen to our son, you must not, whatever else you do, shed a single tear."

He left, and even as Kathleen wondered what he meant, a

great black crow flew through the open window, picked the baby up in its talons and was gone.

At first Kathleen was too shocked to cry. Then she remembered what her husband said and was too strong to weep.

A year passed; another son was born. Kathleen's husband gave the same warning. Even as Kathleen pondered on its meaning, the same crow flew in and snatched the baby away. Still Kathleen shed not a tear.

Another year passed and Kathleen gave birth to a daughter. 'This time I will be lucky and keep the child,' she thought. But no! – again the crow stole the baby. This time, try as she would, Kathleen could not prevent a tear. She caught it in her handkerchief, steeled herself to cry no more and resolved never again to use the handkerchief in which her one tear was trapped.

When he returned, her husband knew – and for the first time since she had known him, was angry.

"One day we shall be sorry you cried!" he shouted.

"I am sorry that I had need to," she answered.

He forgot his anger at once.

After three years, King and Queen O'Hara thought it time they were reunited with their daughters. They invited all three to a great feast. Queen O'Hara watched proudly as two daughters arrived with fine husbands and watched angrily as Kathleen arrived with her dog. When the feast started, Kathleen sat with her dog beside her.

"You can't bring that creature to the table," said Queen O'Hara.

"If he goes, I go" said Kathleen.

"Let the dog stay," said King O'Hara.

Queen O'Hara watched as Kathleen carefully and equally shared all her food with her white dog – and saw also strange expressions she did not understand in the faces of her two elder daughters. She thought, 'I knew there was something strange about the fates of my daughters and I mean to find out what it is.'

That night, while everyone else in the castle slept, Queen O'Hara took a lantern and stole from room to room. She looked in at her first daughter – and saw her alone in bed and a stag sleeping on the floor, its antlers casting weird shadows in the light of the lantern. She tiptoed to the room of her second daughter – and saw that she too was in bed alone while a seal slept by the open window, its wet skin glistening in the moonlight. But in Kathleen's room there was no animal at all. Next to Kathleen lay the handsomest man Queen O'Hara had ever seen.

The Queen's head was reeling. She nearly fainted. She put out her hand to steady herself – and found she was clutching an animal skin. She looked – and saw it was the skin of a great white dog. She snatched it up and ran to the kitchens where fires were being lit for the morning.

"There's bad magic in this castle," she shouted at the servants. "Throw this thing on the fire."

So into the flames went the dogskin. As soon as the fire touched it, there was a shattering noise like twenty rolls of thunder which woke everyone in the castle and for ten miles around. Kathleen's husband woke with the rest. He sat up, saw the skin was gone and with a great cry sprang out of the bed and rushed wildly out of the room, out of the castle and into the country beyond.

Kathleen followed. He ran fast – faster than a dog after a hare, but Kathleen was determined not to lose her husband and somehow she kept him in sight. They ran for a whole day – and as dusk fell, he turned and called to her: "Go back to your father. I'm not for you."

"Never," cried Kathleen. He turned and ran on, and she followed. Twice more he turned and called,

"Go back," and twice more Kathleen answered, "Never."

At last he stopped.

"Kathleen," he said. "I see you are determined so I will have to tell you the truth. If it had not been for your mother you need never have known. If I could have stayed three nights under your parents' roof as your husband I would have become a man both by day and by night."

"How so?" asked Kathleen.

"I and your sisters' husbands come from the Underland. The Queen of the Underland was so enraged that we wanted to leave that she put spells on us stronger even than the magic in your father's cloak. To stay in this world we have to be human half the time, animal the other half – unless we can stay three nights with our wives under their father's roof. Perhaps now the spell is lifted for the other two – for me it is broken beyond mending. The dog half of me is burned and gone so I must go back to the Underland and be slave to the Queen for ever."

"Slave?" said Kathleen.

"I must marry her."

"That's not slavery."

"With her, it's far worse."

"But you're married to me," said Kathleen.

"No more. I'm dead to you. I'll never be seen in this world

again. Goodbye."

He reached for a clump of bulrushes next to him and pulled one. An opening appeared in the ground: he disappeared into it. Without hesitating, Kathleen did the same – and found her world had vanished.

She stood by a river she had never seen before: her husband stood beside her, distraught with anger.

"Why did you do that?" he raved. "I told you to take me as you found me; I told you there was nothing you could do to stop my fate. Now you are ruined as well. While the Queen rules, then once you're here in the Underland, here you stay. There's no going back."

"Then we'll be together," said Kathleen.

"No!" roared her husband. "Don't you understand? I'm bound to the Queen of the Underland."

With that he stalked away. Kathleen, troubled, followed him.

All day they walked. Often, Kathleen's husband turned and cried out to her, "Leave me. Find someone else. I'm no good for you."

"Never!" Kathleen would reply and doggedly follow.

At evening, they saw a cottage.

"Stop here," said the husband. "Go in and ask for shelter. I'll still be outside in the morning."

Kathleen's knock on the door was answered by a gentle-eyed woman who asked her in, gave her food and a bed for the night. As Kathleen gratefully ate her supper by the fire, a little boy ran into the room and tugged her by the hand.

"Mother," he said. "Mother."

The woman of the house took the boy by the hand and led

him gently away. She never mentioned the boy again, nor did Kathleen see him. But in the morning, before Kathleen left, the woman gave her a pair of golden scissors.

"Guard these well," she said, "and they will serve you well. If ever you see a person dressed in rags and you snip at them with these scissors, instantly the rags will turn to clothes of finest cloth of gold. Use these scissors wisely and you may see your son again."

Kathleen thanked her and found her husband outside the house.

"Leave me to my fate," he said.

Kathleen said nothing but continued to follow him. 'After all,' she thought, 'there is nothing to stop him carrying on without her through the night.'

All day they walked. At evening they saw another cottage. Kathleen entered once again to food, warmth, a good bed and the welcome of a kind woman – and once again her husband stayed outside.

As Kathleen ate, again a little boy ran to her and cried, "Mother, mother!" Again he was led gently outside.

But next morning, as she was about to leave, Kathleen was spoken to by the woman of the house.

"Take this silver comb," she said. "Guard it well and it will serve you well. If ever you see a person ill and covered in sores, pass this comb through that person's hair and all will be well. Use this wisely and you may see your son again."

Kathleen thanked her and found her husband still outside the cottage.

"Leave me," he said again.

Kathleen said nothing but followed him as before, wondering

why he had not carried on through the night without her.

All day they walked. Towards evening they reached a third cottage and again Kathleen found welcome from a kind and gentle woman. This time, as Kathleen finished her supper by the fire, a little girl rushed in, threw herself on her lap and cried, "Mother, mother!"

Kathleen could not help herself. She clasped the little girl to her – and gasped in horror at what she saw. The little girl had only one eye – where the other should be was an empty, gaping socket.

"My handkerchief!" she cried – and pulled it out from where it had lain in her pocket untouched since the day she had shed the one tear. She touched the little girl's empty socket with the very spot on the handkerchief where the tear had fallen. At once the socket was filled with a living eye as good as the other one.

The girl ran happily from the room and the woman of the house entered.

"You have done well," she said. She handed Kathleen a little pipe made out of a hazel stem, with holes cut out to make the notes.

"Play a tune on this when you are at your lowest ebb of fortune and you think you've reached the end. Use it wisely and you may see your children again."

Kathleen left the cottage with joy in her heart – and found that this time her husband had not waited for her. She sat on a boulder and burst into tears.

"He has gone without me," she wailed. "He has gone to the Queen of the Underland. I should never have followed him here."

Then she remembered her children that she had thought never to see again and the gifts given to her by the three wise women to smooth her journey. Resolved, she stood up and spoke aloud to the empty air.

"I'll find the queen's castle and him in it and I'll have my way with the lot of them."

So on she walked alone, mile after mile and more and more dispirited, for the horizons in the Underland seemed as far away as they did in her old world. She followed the river as it wound along its rushy banks until, at nightfall, she saw in front of her a massive, gloomy, forbidding castle. She shivered with fear for in it, she knew without any doubt, lived her dreadful rival the Queen of the Underland.

She could go no further. By the river she found yet another cottage. In it lived a washerwoman.

"Shelter me and I'll work for you for nothing," said Kathleen and the washerwoman gladly agreed.

Next day the two women were beating out washing on the riverbank when a fanfare of trumpets sounded from the castle.

"What is that?" said Kathleen.

"The Queen marries today," replied the washerwoman.

"Who does she marry?"

"A man who has been to the upper world and is under her spell. He'll not last any longer than all her other husbands."

Kathleen said nothing, but pounded the washing with new force.

Near the washerwoman's cottage lived a henwife who kept poultry for the queen. Her small son, dressed in filthy rags, ran over to where Kathleen was working and she looked in surprise at the miserable sight he presented.

"You poor thing," she cried and pulled out her golden scissors. She snipped with them at the rags – and at once the boy was wearing a tunic of cloth of gold which gleamed in the sunlight.

The boy looked at Kathleen. Kathleen looked at the boy. Then, with a whoop of joy he ran back to his mother.

But his mother was not pleased.

"How did you come by that?" she demanded.

"There's a lady in the washerwoman's house who has a magic pair of scissors."

The henwife worked for the queen and, though poor, was loyal. She walked up to the castle and spoke to the queen even though the wedding feast was still on.

"There's someone new in the Underland who works magic," she said. "If I were you I'd get rid of her but keep her scissors."

The queen stopped eating.

"Tell her to hand the scissors to me. If not, I'll have her beheaded."

The henwife brought Kathleen the message. Kathleen sent a message back.

"I will give up my scissors if I can have one night with the man who is my husband, not yours."

"I accept," came the surprising answer back.

But when Kathleen came to her husband that night she found he was stretched out on his back, snoring. The queen had drugged him. Kathleen waited all night but he never stirred. Next morning she sorrowfully returned to the washerwoman.

As she was working that morning by the river, the henwife's daughter came to her. She was s sickly girl, thin as a rake with her body covered in sores.

"Oh, you poor thing," gasped Kathleen. Without thinking, she took out her comb and ran it through the girl's sparse hair. At once, she had a beautiful, thick mass of golden curls. Her skin was clear and she was no longer skin and bone. She ran joyfully back to her mother who took one look and was not pleased.

"What's happened to you?" she said.

"The lady who lives with the washerwoman has a magic comb," the girl replied.

At once the henwife went to the queen.

"The woman has a magic comb as well. Get it from her or she'll be your rival."

The message came back to Kathleen: "Give up the comb or lose your head."

The answer returned: "The comb is yours in return for another night with my husband."

But once again the husband was drugged and Kathleen watched over an unconscious form. When morning came, Kathleen never went back to the washerwoman's house. Soldiers came, hustled her down to a dungeon and clanged the iron door shut.

"Your head will be off by the day's end," said one.

Kathleen crouched miserably in a dark corner of the dripping dungeon. For hours she waited. Then, in late afternoon, she heard a whisper.

"Kathleen."

She looked up. There, looking through the bars of the tiny window, was her husband.

"Kathleen," he said. "What are we to do? The Queen has made me marry her so now I am nothing but her slave. When you are beheaded, she will put a spell of forgetfulness on me so all my past life will disappear. We've reached the end, you and I."

Then Kathleen remembered. She had a third object: the little pipe made from a hazel twig. She took it out, put it to her lips and played a sad little tune.

At once, the dungeon was full of birds and sun streamed in through the barred window through which they had flown. A dove perched on Kathleen's wrist and spoke to her.

"We bring you the queen's closest secret. There's only one person in the Underland who can kill her and that's her husband. And there's only one way he can do it."

"Tell me," said Kathleen's husband.

"In the courtyard of the castle is a holly tree. Deep in that tree there is an egg. Inside that egg the queen keeps both her heart and her life, where none can reach them. And only the queen's husband can take an axe to that tree."

"But how can we get out of the castle to do it?" moaned Kathleen's husband.

Kathleen said nothing, but blew the whistle again. At once, the door of the dungeon burst open and in her husband's hands was a huge, shining axe.

They marched together out of the dungeon, through the castle and into the courtyard. The flock of birds flew overhead and nobody tried to stop them. There stood the gnarled old holly tree, its branches like stiff, barbed arms warding them off. Kathleen's husband drew the axe back and took a mighty swing. Thwack!

The axe bit deep into the tree, but it did not move.

Another mighty swing. Thud!

This time the tree shook slightly.

A third blow, even stronger than the other two.

Now, with a creak and a shriek that sounded like a human cry, the tree split open. There, nestling deep inside the trunk, was a white egg. Without hesitating, Kathleen's husband smashed it. The white and the yolk spilled out and merged and soaked away into the ground. As it did so, there came from the castle a long, terrifying howl of rage, pain and defeat which gradually died away into silence.

Kathleen and her husband stood still for some time.

"You have won," said the dove, and all the birds flew away.

"We're free," said Kathleen's husband. "All her enchantments are gone."

Kathleen looked beyond the courtyard. Three children – two boys and a girl – were running towards her. She bent down and swept them up into her arms.

"We'll reign together in the Underland as king and queen," said her husband. "For ever and ever."

But Kathleen thought, "All the enchantments are gone now and there's King and Queen O'Hara and my two sisters and their husbands in the upper world in Ireland and that's where my home is."

So she looked at her husband and said, "Use me wisely, husband, so I may see my family again. Otherwise, the story may not be over."

THE FAR ISLAND

Two fishermen talked about Faeryland. They sat by a roaring fire in a stout, stone croft on dry land as heavy seas crashed outside in the night and harsh gales howled and moaned over the bleak shore. The fire warmed their bodies and the good whisky warmed their insides. Lachlan from Orkney and Roderick from Shetland sat each side of the hearth. The firelight made shadows leap across the walls as they talked of Faeryland.

"A place where you're never hungry," said Lachlan.

"A place where the fish crowd into your nets so they are full to bursting," said Roderick.

"Where the sun shines and no gales chill you to the marrow and break up your frail boat as you sail it," said Lachlan.

"There is such a place," said Roderick. "If only I dare look for it."

"I know someone who has been there."

"Do you? So do I."

"And from what happened to him I'm not sure I want to know where Faeryland is."

"But the one I know who came back is the better for it."

"Ah, but was it the same place that he went to?"

"Tell me and I will see."

"I will," said Lachlan from Orkney. He refilled their mugs from the jug. Then he took a long swallow of his whisky, looked into the fire as if Faeryland lay inside it and started.

"This was some years ago now and it was Lammas Fair in Kirkwall. My story is about Tam Scott from the Isle of Sanday, to the east of Kirkwall. He worked his parley boat and took folk from the isle to the town whenever they wanted and today his craft had been full because it was Lammas Fair.

"Well, Tam Scott had landed his people and had the whole day to himself until it was time for them to board again. He was having a great time what with the dancing and the drinking and the laughing when all at once he saw a man he had never seen before and who made him stop in his tracks. A tall man with a thin face the colour of parchment, high cheekbones which made it look caved in and a chin so pointed you could nearly spear fish with it. A man wearing a dusty black cloak which swished along the ground behind him. A man with, hanging round his neck, a little silver box with a tiny key which Tam thought must hold his snuff.

"Tam looked at him and the man looked at Tam and Tam found he couldn't move a muscle. But when the man spoke, Tam nearly fell off the quay and into the water with shock.

"'Good day to you, Tam Scott. And a very good day it is indeed for you, for today you will work for me and for no one else.'

"Tam recovered his wits quickly.

"'I'll work for anybody who pays me fairly,' he said. 'But I work best when I know the name of my employer.'

"'This time there is no need for you to know anything about who employs you,' said the man. 'Except that he pays three times the going rate for a job well done.'

"Tam was no fool.

"'That suits me fine,' he said.

"'Then have your boat made ready at the far end of the quay and I'll meet you there in one hour.'

"Making ready did not take Tam long. An hour later he was waiting at the end of the quay – and, on the dot, there was the dark stranger. He was leading a fine black milch cow.

"'We're to take this cow I've paid good money for to an island to the north-east of here. I'll guide your course.'

"'Which island?' said Tam, who knew them all.

"'You do not need to know. Just do as I say.'

"And with that, to Tam's amazement, the stranger lifted up the cow as if it had been a kitten and placed it in the stern of the boat.

"'Now, set sail,' he said.

"The day was fine and the breeze was strong. They soon cleared Kirkwall harbour and Tam said, 'Now where?'

"'To Shapinshay.'

"Tam thought to himself: 'Not so far after all.' But when they reached Shapinshay, the stranger said, 'Now bear east and make for Stronsay.'

"That's not too bad. When the coast of Stronsay came near he said, 'We'll land in Mill Bay.'

"'We will not,' said the stranger. 'Steer east and make for Sanday.'

"'I'm home already,' thought Tam. 'I'll go back for the others later.'

"When the coast of Sanday came in sight, Tam asked 'Where do we land here?'

"Nowhere," said the stranger. 'Steer east and then north.'

"'But ...' began Tam.

"The stranger tapped the little silver box hanging round his neck. 'Ask no questions. He who knows least, fears least.'

"Tam looked again at the dark stranger and found that though he knew nothing, he suddenly feared greatly. He thought he had taken on board a man like himself and now he realised that instead the frail planks of his craft were trodden by some ghoulish creature from another world. And now the boat was headed for the open sea for which it was not built and where Tam had never been.

"'Northwards now,' said the man. 'Ever northwards.'

"Now the sun began to set but still the boat drove on. Tam was deeply frightened. The stranger sat silent, staring forward, his black eyes unblinking. At last Tam saw a bank of dense mist in front of him.

"'Keep on,' said the stranger.

"Tam steered straight into the cold, wet fog. He sat shivering at the tiller and could not see his own hand gripping it. He was terrified.

"'Straight ahead,' said the stranger.

"Then, suddenly, they were in sunlight. Tam stared amazed. For in front of him was an island of sandy beaches and soft green hills. On the lower slopes were cornfields yellow with full harvests. Tall trees and carpets of bright flowers lined them. As his boat drew nearer, Tam saw people flocking to the shore: fair, strong, beautiful people looking out to sea and watching him with grave and serious faces.

"The stranger spoke again. 'Now I must blindfold you. Do as I say and all will be well.'

"Tam didn't like this.

"'Why? This is a wonderful place. Why shouldn't I see it?'

"'Do as I say!'

"There was a threat in the stranger's voice. So Tam let himself be blindfolded.

"The boat drove on. Tam felt the shock and heard the scrunch as the prow dug into pebbles and sand. He heard voices – clear, high, melodious voices as the people helped the stranger and his cow off the boat.

"Then Tam heard a sound such as he could never have imagined even in his dreams: singing so pure and perfect that his heart nearly stopped. 'Whose voices are these? I must see,' he thought. He lifted the blindfold and snatched a glance towards where the melody came from. He caught his breath with ecstasy.

"He saw a little cove bounded by rocks. On the rocks sat mermaids with lovely faces and long yellow hair who leaned forward and beckoned him. Tam lunged forward into a run towards them.

"But the stranger had seen. He pulled the blindfold roughly back over Tam's head and shouted to the mermaids: 'You'll never lure this man away to you. Why, he has a wife and children on Orkney and no man could leave them to their own devices for a pretty voice and a fish's tail.'

"The song changed at once to a mournful lament and Tam's heart was full of misery.

"'You've done what you came for and there's an end of it,' the stranger's voice said. 'So here's your money. Now get out.'

"Tam heard the clunk of a heavy bag full of coins landing in the boat. He felt the boat being pushed away and the sudden lightness as it floated.

"'Tell no one what you've seen,' came the stranger's voice. 'Or you'll be sorry.'

"'And steer straight ahead,' came other voices. 'You'll soon make land.'

"Tam tore the blindfold away. He was once again in thick fog, without bearings, sure he was lost. He tried to steer a straight course, but the fog persisted and he had no idea where he was. Then, suddenly, it lifted – and Tam, in bright sunlight, saw his own familiar coast.

"Well, Tam was a sociable soul and couldn't keep anything to himself. Many were the friends to whom he told his strange tale: many were the friends who didn't believe a word of it.

"'I'll prove it to you one day,' he said as he bought them drinks with the money the island folk had paid him.

"But he had to wait until next Lammas Fair for a chance. He was with a crowd of friends on the quayside when he saw him again the dark stranger with the cloak and the silver snuffbox hanging round his neck.

"'That's the man,' cried Tam. 'Now I'll prove it to you.'

"He went up to the stranger. 'Hello there! Are there any more cows for me to take to Faeryland?'

"'You have never seen me before,' said the man.

"'Of course I have. And I've worked for you.'

"'I see that you have told what you should not.'

"'Only to a few friends. Where's the harm in that?'

"'I say that not only have you never seen me before but I will make sure you never see me again.'

"He stepped right up to Tam and stared him in the face. Tam blinked. Then the stranger lifted the silver box hung round his neck, turned the key and opened the lid. He held the box under Tam's nose and blew powder from it into Tam's eyes.

"'Now whatever you see is only in your mind,' he said.

"And he was right. For when the screaming Tam could open

his eyes after the terrible, burning pain he realised he was blind. And he stayed blind until his dying day. No one, blind or not, ever met the dark stranger again at Lammas Fair in Kirkwall."

Lachlan poured more whisky into his mug and refilled Roderick's as well.

"Ah," said Roderick. "That's a hard tale to hear. But the faery folk are not always so ill-disposed to humankind. I'll prove it to you."

"Tell away," said Lachlan. "I'll be pleased to hear it."

"My tale," said Roderick, "is of two young fishermen from Lunna, close to where I live in Shetland. Thom and Willie they were called, and two better friends you could not have – until, that is, they both fell in love with Osla, Jarm's daughter. Then the friendship between them cooled, I can tell you.

"But they still worked together and one October day they set sail and had a good catch. Then, as they were turning for home, the wind rose and soon they were in a roaring gale. They clung on for dear life and just as they thought they were lost the gale dropped. They found themselves in calm seas but – as with Tam Scott – in thick fog. Like him, they lost all sense of direction and, like him, they unexpectedly found themselves when the fog cleared in sunlight and close to an island. This, though, was no paradise with mermaids. This was rocky, bare and inhospitable. As there was nowhere else to go they landed, drew the boat up the beach and found shelter in a cave. Thom curled up at once and slept. Willie prowled around agitatedly because a plan had come into his mind – a plan so wicked that it scared him. If he could sail the boat back home on his own, nobody would ever find Thom again. He would starve to death in this desolate place and Osla would have no choice: Willie would be her husband.

"The more Willie thought about this, the better the plan seemed. He made up a dreadful tale of Thom being lost overboard in the gale and his own heroic attempts to save his best friend. He took a look in at the cave and saw Thom sleeping soundly and innocently – and made his mind up. He dragged the boat down to the water, jumped in and set sail for Lunna.

"Well, Thom woke with the dawn, called Willie, got no answer, rushed to the beach – and found how he had been tricked. He knew he was finished. No food, no water – death was certain.

"What could he do? Nothing. So he went back into the shelter of the cave and tried to sleep again and wait for his death the best way he could.

"Meanwhile, Willie made good progress home. When he landed, he rushed into the village, shouting: 'My best friend is drowned. We'll never see our Thom again.' Everyone was grieved for Thom but full of praise for Willie's brave but hopeless efforts. Osla was heartbroken.

"Days, weeks and months went by and at length she allowed Willie and Jarm together to persuade her that she now had no choice about who to marry.

"Back on the island, on his first full night after a day picking his way through stony rubbish, Thom curled up as best he could, shivering in the cave. He dozed in snatches and finally slept the dreamless sleep of complete hopelessness.

"He must have slept for six hours when he found himself sitting up, every nerve awake. Something extraordinary had roused him. What? He could hear music, he could see soft light. He looked round. The cave was gone: he sat on the smooth, marble floor of a rich and beautiful banqueting hall. Long tables stretched the length of this high, vaulted, decorated chamber. At the far end was a raised stage with a colourful canopy and a sumptuously laid table. The music grew louder. In walked a procession of tiny people, brightly dressed and wearing shining jewels. They took their places at the long tables and looked towards the raised dais at the far end. The music changed to a stately fanfare and in walked two impressive figures: a man and a woman, wearing silver crowns and white robes edged with gold. They stood at their places at the high table. The music stopped, they nodded and the whole host sat.

"Thom watched, amazed. He knew he must be at a faery feast and that the forbidding, imperious couple sitting at the top table were the Faery King and the Faery Queen. He looked longingly at the food the faeries were eating. How hungry he was! He couldn't help himself. He stood up and rushed forward to grasp a pie on the nearest table.

"At once, all the faeries stopped eating and turned to him. He felt their eyes boring into his: he felt every secret in his mind was now theirs. Then, without any warning, he was plunged into darkness. The scene had vanished and he was back in the cold cave where the wind moaned and dankness entered his bones.

"'It was a dream' he said aloud. 'Now I'm really done for.'

"He tried to sleep again, but it was no use. Hours later, the cave was lit by daylight. Thom looked despairingly round him – and gasped in amazement.

"Yes, the hall, the tables, the faeries themselves were all gone, but the food was still there, pies, legs of lamb, pork and beef; chickens, geese; bread, all sorts of fruit, cheese. Enough to keep a man alive and eating well for months. Jugs of whisky and strong ale, so no thirst and constant happiness. But wait. What was he always told about faery food? That it was tasteless, bitter: that it was fatal to humans because they would either die or become faeries themselves.

"'I'm going to die anyway,' reasoned Thom. 'So either that or I'll be a faery myself. I can't lose.' So he chose the very pie he had tried to grab the night before. He bit ravenously into it. The pastry was light and delicious; the filling was like food for the gods themselves.

"He swallowed his first mouthful. He neither died nor felt like anything but the Thom he had always been.

"'Of course,' he said aloud. 'I knew the faeries saw into my very soul. They realised why I was here. They took pity on me.'

"So he looked for driftwood to make a fire and prepared to be as comfortable on the island as he could for as long as he needed.

"The day of Osla's marriage to Willie was near. But Osla was unhappy. She dreamt night after night of Thom. The dreams were so real – she kept seeing Thom living alone on a rocky island, looking out to sea day after day for a boat to come and rescue him.

"She told Thom's parents.

"'Ah, you poor lassie,' they said. 'It's wishful thinking. Our dear son's drowned. Willie tried to rescue him like the good friend he is but even he wasn't strong enough to stop him going overboard in the gale. Forget Thom. He's gone for ever.'

"'I don't believe it,' said Osla and kept talking about her dreams to all who would listen until her father lost patience.

"'All right, girl,' he said. 'You and I will search the islands together just to show you Thom's never coming back.'

"So he and Osla set sail in his boat. They combed the islands and found nothing.

"'You see?' said her father and turned for home.

"Towards evening a mist descended. Soon they were enveloped in thick fog.

"'We're lost,' cried Jarm angrily. 'Now look what you've led me into!'

"Osla stayed calm.

"'Just wait, father,' she said.

"The mist cleared. They were close to the shore of an island. Jarm steered the boat into a rocky bay. And before its prow burrowed into the shingle a figure scrambled down the rocks. Osla saw her dreams were true and her beloved Thom was alive. So they set sail for Lunna and when they reached home the joy was unconfined."

"But what about Willie?" said Lachlan.

"Willie was a broken man. Seen as a cheat and nearly a murderer, he was shunned by everybody. He didn't last long: one day he sailed off in his boat and that was the last anyone saw of him."

"To the faery isle, do you think?"

"If he did, you can be sure there was no food left out for him."

Lachlan was silent. Then he said, "The faeries may be cruel but deep down I suppose they are fair."

"I would not want to risk their anger," said Roderick. "I would not want to be blinded, like your Tam."

"But I would like the wrongs righted that were done to me," said Lachlan. "As was done for your Thom."

Roderick looked deep into the fire as it glowed red.

"It occurs to me," he said, "that you know the course Tam Scott took from Kirkwall. And I could trace the course Thom and Willie sailed from Lunna. Together we could find Faeryland."

Lachlan thought of feasts of gorgeous food, more than he could eat, and drink to keep him warm for the rest of his life.

"You're right," he said. "We could."

Roderick thought of sunlight, yellow corn, green hills and mermaids singing.

"The wind has dropped," he said. "We'll go now."

But as they stepped out on to the beach, other visions came into their minds – Tam Scott blinded; the starved body of Willie stretched out on rocks for gulls to peck at. They turned back.

"There's heat in the fire and whisky in the jug," said Lachlan. "And more tales to tell."

"And I'm for all three after all," said Roderick.

ELIDOR RETURNS

Elidor knew a lot of stories by now. How different they all were. The King of the Underland was right – "Strange, is it not, how mortals see us?" So was the queen – "You mortals, whenever you find us, must make of us what you will."

Was this king he had spoken to the same king who once fought Havgan every year, who stole Heurodis and then was charmed by Orfeo's music, who ran a desperate race for survival every seven years? Well, there was surely only one Underland so there could only be one king of it. When Elidor first entered the castle, he had passed the very gatehouse where the porter had seen Orfeo's wild appearance yet still had let him in. When he stood at the entrance to the great hall he had been where Pwll, in the guise of Arawn, had first seen the queen – that same queen who told Elidor he would be playmate for her son and yet had screamed aloud at the loss of Tam Lin.

So everyone had indeed seen them differently. Besides, where was the Underland? In Wales? Scotland? England? Ireland? Or was it everywhere? And what about time there? Elidor knew time was different in the two worlds. That's why his mother never knew he had been away. Oisin knew it was different as well. But had it been different for Pwll? Or Orfeo? Orfeo had aged in the wild lands: was Heurodis ten years older when she came back to Winchester?

Elidor could not answer these questions. But night after night he talked to his mother about where he had been and where he must soon return. Gradually she came to believe him. She asked him more and more questions about the Underland. He described all the things he had seen and her eyes grew dreamy.

"I wish I could go there," she said one night.

"You couldn't squeeze through the passage," he replied.

"Tell me about the game you play," she said.

"Oh, not the marbles again," said Elidor.

She always wanted to hear about the faery children at play: he was getting tired of explaining. But once again he wearily went through it.

"And the marbles are like big golden apples," he said as he finished.

Usually when he reached this point his mother just nodded, closed her eyes and dozed off. But tonight she did not.

"I've been doing some thinking too," she said. "Do you know what I believe? They are apples."

"So what?" said Elidor.

"Not just any apples. *The* apples. The golden apples of immortality."

"The what?" said Elidor.

"I heard about them years ago from my grandmother. And she had it from hers; a story that's been told for thousands of years. The golden apples of immortality were stolen from the gods at the dawn of time by giants who came to live in Britain long before the first humans arrived. The giants hid the apples and no one knows where. But you have found them. They were in the Underland all the time."

"But what are they?" said Elidor.

"Take one bite of them and you will never die," said his mother.

"Rubbish," said Elidor.

"What did the queen's son say when you wanted to eat one?"

Elidor thought. Then he said, wonderingly and slowly, "Humans who eat these lose the one thing that makes them human."

"You see?" said his mother. "The one thing that makes us human is that we die. The faeries don't need to eat the apples."

"Why not?"

"Because they are immortal already. Oh, Elidor" – and here she leaned forward, eyes shining, and clasped his hands – "next time you come to visit me, bring a golden apple with you."

"Why?"

"I want to be immortal."

Elidor looked round the mean shack they lived in and at the remains of the miserable stew and the lumps of stale bread. He felt the cold wind piercing through the holes in the walls.

"Why?" he repeated.

"*Please!*" she said.

Elidor remembered something else the king had said: "'Never take anything from here away with you and never bring anything back'."

"I can't," he said.

"But you can," his mother replied. "Hide it in your clothes. No one will know."

She was so insistent: at last Elidor promised.

Next day he left home again: down the hill, into the woods, through the cave, along the tunnel and back in the warm sunlight and the soft grass of the lush meadows.

Everybody seemed pleased to see him. He had no idea how long they thought he had been away. The king and queen received him politely and graciously – and this time fed him well. When he was full, their son and the other children delightedly took him away to the sunlit garden to play.

So began another magical time of playing, eating, lazing in the sun and sailing down wide rivers in boats with silken sails. Happiness and ease stretched out for as long as he wanted it. He lost track of time. But he never forgot the stories of others who had been there before him. Sometimes he explored the Underland to find places he had heard of. He looked for the hill with the throne of stones at the summit, up which Oisin had raced Mannanan. Sometimes he sought the ford where Pwll had fought Havgan. Sometimes, with fear tugging at his heart lest he should find it, he searched for the dump of the dead that Orfeo passed. He found none of them.

In the end, he forgot these things and gave himself up to lazy pleasure. The children still played marbles with the golden apples and often Elidor picked one of them up, felt its smooth skin and its slight softness and wondered what would happen if he took a bite. But he never did and if the temptation ever nearly became too strong there was always someone at hand to shout, "Don't!"

At length, though, homesickness came again. It was time to go back to the world of mortals. He told the king.

"Very well," was the reply. "But remember, take nothing with you."

Elidor felt a stab of guilt: he had been trying to forget his promise to his mother.

"Of course I won't," he said, but he knew he lied.

From then on, he never had a moment's peace. When they played marbles, he now and then slipped golden apples into pockets in his tunic to see which looked least obvious. The very smallest – no more than a crab apple – left no sign at all. That apple he decided to steal. No one, he was sure, knew what he was doing.

Elidor decided to leave immediately after an afternoon's playing. He said his farewells to everyone – "But I'll be back soon," he insisted. Carefully, while no one was looking, he slipped the smallest apple into his tunic. Then he walked away from the castle, along the river, up through the meadows and into the tunnel.

Here he found a difficulty. The tunnel was such a tight squeeze that he couldn't keep the apple in his pocket: as well as hurting himself he would squash it. So he took it out and held it in his hand. Now he inched his way along the tunnel with the hand clutching the apple extended in front of him.

It was very dark in the tunnel. Had he grown since he first came? Crawling down it was slower and harder than before. He could hear voices all round him – as if the faery folk were following. This time he could make out no words – but he felt menaced in some way he didn't understand. The sounds did not grow fainter as he drew further away: they grew louder and so close that they seemed to be coming from inside his own head.

At last he was in the cave. It was still pitch dark. Elidor stood up. Where was the entrance? He was sure he had always been able to see it from here. The apple was still in his hand. He wondered whether to put it in his pocket. No. He couldn't see, so it was best to keep hold of it.

He took a step in what he hoped was the right direction.

Then another; then another. He began to gain in confidence. Was that a pale glow of light ahead? He took a pace towards it.

Suddenly he was falling – on to the rough, rocky floor of the cave. He clung hard to the apple. As he struggled to get up again, he felt as if he was held down by hundreds of tiny hands and little fingers of immense strength seemed to be prising his own fingers apart. Soon he knew the apple was gone. He groped wildly round for it. No use.

Voices sounded all round him. There was nothing tinkly or musical about them.

"Take nothing away! Take nothing away!" – the grating chant filled his ears.

Then there was silence. The cave exit stood bright in front of him. Elidor ran through it and back home to confess to his mother what had happened.

She was distraught.

"I asked you to do just one little thing for me," she cried. "It was so easy, but you messed it up,"

"It wasn't my fault," said Elidor.

"You must have just dropped it on the floor of the cave," said his mother. "Light a fire in the cave: then you'll see it."

"I'll try," said Elidor.

Next day he went to the place where the cave was. When he got there, he stared.

Bare earth, rocks, tree roots twisting on the surface: no cave. He searched desperately. There was no sign that there had ever been a cleft in the ground.

He ran back home.

"It's gone," he wailed. "The cave is sealed up."

"Hmm," said his mother. "Was it ever there, I wonder?"

"I'm banished from Faeryland for ever!" Elidor howled in anguish.

"My poor boy," said his mother. Was there a sarcastic edge to her voice? "Well, after an experience like that, you'll never be any good working the farm now. You'll never be able to keep your mind on what you're doing. Leave all that to your brothers. From now on, the monastery's all you're fit for."

So to the monastery Elidor went. He became a monk and lived to a great age. All his life, he told the story to anyone who would listen of how when he was a boy he found the way into the Underland and tried to steal the golden apples. Some said he was mad, others listened and believed. A few went looking for the entrance to the Underland hoping they might have the same great adventures as Elidor – and Pwll, Orfeo, Oisin, Tam Lin, Kathleen before him.

But no one found the entrance again, so no one did. As far as I know, no one ever has.